THE RED CARDIGAN

J.C.BURKE

RANDOM HOUSE AUSTRALIA

For David Burke: writer, mentor, editor, friend – father.

Random House Australia Pty Ltd
20 Alfred Street, Milsons Point, NSW 2061
http://www.randomhouse.com.au
Sydney   New York   Toronto
London   Auckland   Johannesburg

First published by Random House Australia 2004
Copyright © J. C. Burke 2004

National Library of Australia
Cataloguing-in-Publication Entry
    Burke, J. C.
    The red cardigan.
    For secondary students.
    ISBN 0 7593 2029 2.
    1. Clairvoyance - Fiction. I. Title.
    A823.4

Cover and internal design by Mathematics
Typeset in Deepdene by Midland Typesetters
Printed and bound by The SOS Print and Media Group

10 9 8 7 6 5 4 3 2

Verse on p.189 from *The Rime of the Ancient Mariner* (Part 6)
by Samuel Taylor Coleridge (1772-1834).

Lyrics on p.38 from *New Year's Prayer* by Jeff Buckley © 1998,
used by permission of Sony Music. All rights reserved.

What is a friend? A single soul dwelling in two bodies.

ARISTOTLE

PART ONE

She searches for the smell. She finds it – the sweet perfume of a Murraya bush in summer. It's the only memory of her grandfather and it's still exactly as it was. She is sitting on his knee in an old green kitchen. A loose thread hangs from his singlet. Winding it around her finger, she listens to him speak.

'Your gran knows things, Evie.'

She nods.

'Sometimes,' his voice drops to a whisper, 'sometimes she knows things before they've even happened.'

Today, Evie turns this memory over and over, trying to hear each word as if for the first time. She needs to fill in the gaps, make sense of something she knows she cannot ask others. Somehow she understands dark times lie ahead. This is who she is. This is her curse.

At recess Alex watches her. 'Are you okay, Evie?'

'Yeah,' agrees Poppy. 'You look kind of – weird.'

Evie sees Alex mouth 'shut up', but doesn't care. She wants to go home. She needs to be alone. 'I feel like I'm going to spew.'

Poppy jumps behind Alex. 'What? Now?'

'I think I'll go up to the office and see if I can go home.'

Alex and Poppy glance at each other.

'Do you really think that's, um – a good idea?'

'You're sounding like my mother, Alex.' Evie fiddles with the buttons on her cuff. It's best not to look at them. 'I'm okay. I just feel sick.'

'Want us to come to the office with you?'

'I'll be fine. See you tomorrow.'

Evie walks briskly through a draughty corridor leading to the school office. 'The walk of shame' the students call it. Shivering, she pulls her cardigan around her chest. The cardigan is crimson red and made from the softest wool. Her dad brought it back from Adelaide, last week. He'd picked it up at a vintage store near where he'd stayed. 'Impulse buying,' he'd grinned. Evie never lets on, but she understands why he spoils her. It helps relieve his guilt.

Usually she feels good wearing the cardigan to school. Red is the regulation colour for jumpers at Goulburn Street Girls' High but Evie's cardigan is vintage. She saw the 'cool girls' or, as Alex calls them, 'the CGs' eyeing it off at morning assembly. But now she wants to escape their prying eyes, in case they notice, too.

Outside, heavy black clouds sit low in the sky. Evie doesn't have to look up; she feels them crowding her space, sucking her air. She wishes she could push them away, up where they belong. But today she lacks the strength. It's all she can do just to keep it together.

'Thank god,' she sighs, closing the front door. 'Home and alone.'

Thursday is her mum's university teaching day. If it wasn't, Evie would have stayed at school – anything to avoid her mother's frown and pursed lips. It's been ages since Evie's had a bad day. She figures no one needs to know about this one.

She climbs the stairs to her bedroom, takes off her cardigan and goes to hang it over the chair. Hiding inside the shoulder seam is a tiny knot of hair. She pulls it out and holds it up to the light. It's the colour of dark copper.

A sharp pain strikes the back of Evie's head. She slumps onto the bed trying to catch her breath. Her throat is making a rasping noise that sounds like it's coming from the other side of the room. She buries herself under the doona. It's safer in the dark.

'Not again,' she moans. 'Pleeease, not again.'

'Muuum?' Evie calls from the laundry. 'I can't find any socks and I need you to sign a note.'

'Evie! Don't just chuck everything out of the clean washing basket.' Her mum sighs. 'What do you want? Socks?'

'There's none here.' Evie stuffs the clothes back in the basket.

'Give me the basket. I folded all this stuff last night and I'm not doing it again.'

'Come on, Evie,' her dad calls from the kitchen. 'We've got to go.'

'Okay, okay.'

'Have you looked in the dryer?' her mother snaps.

'No. I haven't,' she snaps back.

'Hurry up, Evie. I've got a press conference this morning.'

'Hang on, Dad. I'm coming.'

'Here.' Evie's mother thrusts a pair of socks in her face.

Evie hops to the kitchen trying to put the socks on while

her mother stuffs things into her school bag.

'For godsakes, Evie. Sit down and put your socks on properly.'

If there's one piece of public knowledge in the Simmons's household, it's that Nick Simmons, Evie's father and Executive Producer of Radio News, cannot under any circumstances be late for a press conference.

'What was the other thing you needed?' Her mother is fighting with the bag's zipper and isn't winning.

'Evie, you've got to be more organised.' Now her dad's on the case. 'You're in Year 12 next year. You know, final exams and all that stuff.'

'Nick, be quiet,' her mum says. 'Evie, did you say I had to sign something?'

'Yeah.'

Evie takes the note out of her pocket. She has folded it, just to show the dotted line where a signature is required.

She points, 'Just sign there.'

Nick is walking to the front door. Evie picks up her bag with one hand, still holding the note firmly in the other. Her mother takes the corner of the note but Evie won't let go. She tugs at it and Evie's grip tightens.

'Evie!' Her mother prises it out from her daughter's fingers, unfolding her secret.

'What?' She watches her mother's expression slide down her face into her jaw. 'You what? You left school at recess?'

'Yeah.'

Evie reaches out her hand but her mother holds the note to her chest.

'Were you – sick?'

Evie nods.

'You didn't tell us that last night.' Nick has put down his briefcase and is walking towards her. 'Are you okay?'

'I'm fine.'

'Sure?'

'Yes, Dad, I'm sure.'

'She looks okay to me. Don't you think, Nick?' Her mother's knuckles turn white as she crumples the note in her hand.

Evie looks at her shoes. 'Can we – um – go now?'

'Sure you don't want to tell us anything?'

'No, Dad. For the one billioneth time, I'm fine. Okay?'

'Great.' He puts his hand on her shoulder. 'The cardigan suits you. Doesn't it, Robin?'

'Thanks, Dad.'

Her mother smooths out the note and hands it back. 'Next time, I'd appreciate it if you called me. I thought we agreed you'd tell us if anything was . . . going on.'

'I will. I just felt sick. No big deal.'

Her mother nods. 'Good.'

But Evie knows her mother doesn't believe her.

She holds her breath until she's out the gate and in her dad's car. His press conference has saved her from answering the full encyclopedia of questions her mother was probably busting to ask. She knows how they begin and how they end. And the tone, the suspicious tone! Doesn't her mother know how obvious it is? Evie shakes her head.

7

'What?' Nick asks.

'Nothing.'

Her father's actions and words have slowed from the morning's rush. It's not that he's relaxed – she knows that by the way he wipes his hands on his pants leaving a smudge on the fabric. This is him trying to act cool and unfazed, always conscious of his role as the middleman.

'So what have you got first?' he asks, reaching back for his seatbelt.

'Art.'

She watches his grip on the steering wheel tighten. 'Are you, um, working on anything yet?'

'Well, I have to start on ideas for my major work.'

'Okay.' He clears his throat and slowly says, 'And what are you thinking of?'

Evie must choose her words carefully. Not enough time has passed. She knows he still hurts. Don't they all.

'Well,' she swallows. 'I'm still desperate to do a composition of portraits. You know I've always wanted to do that for my major work. And I . . . I still think I can.'

Silence.

'Alex has offered to be my subject.'

'Really?'

'There's just one proviso.'

'What's that?'

'That I don't include any zits on her face.'

'But that's texture.' He laughs a bit too loud. He can't hide his relief.

'Dad! Alex'd die if she heard you say that.'

'Then don't tell her.'

'As if.'

'What's Al doing for her major work?'

'Photography.' They say it at the same time.

'Jinx,' laughs Evie. 'Dad, it's Alex's cheekbones. They're so angular. They're like these rocks jutting out of a cliff face, and her eyes are really deep set. They'll be tricky but I reckon –'

'Darling, it'll be great seeing you draw again.'

'I'm not sure Mr Powell or Mum agree with that, Dad.'

He doesn't reply. Evie stares out the window, watching the rows of terraces fold into one another.

'So, what's the big press conference about?'

'Bob Garling, the Commissioner of Police, is making an announcement.'

'I bet that'll be earth shattering.'

'They're increasing the number of uniformed police on public transport.'

'Bit late for that.'

'Well, yes and no.' He toots at the car in front. 'Come on! The police have to be seen to be doing something.'

'Do you think it would have stopped that girl from being raped?'

'Who knows?'

As Evie gets out of the car, her dad leans over and squeezes her arm. 'You're our most precious possession you know? We just – worry, if you . . .'

'I'm fine, Dad. Okay?'

Evie holds her breath and looks up to a clear winter sky

that goes on and on. Today is a new day. She feels certain she'll be left alone.

Evie and Alex sit together in art class. Evie is holding Alex's chin, tilting it backwards and forwards, looking for an interesting angle.

'That's such a cool cardi, Evie.'

'Yes, you can borrow it.'

'I don't think red's my colour,' Alex says, her face turned upwards, her mousey hair squashed under the creases of her neck. 'I think powder blue with beads is more me. Don't you?'

'What are you after?'

'Can I wear it to Taylor's party next weekend? Please, please?'

'Are you going to Taylor's party?'

'Well, I'm thinking of it.'

Evie lets go of Alex's chin and starts sketching some lines.

'How about you?'

'No.' Evie doesn't look up.

'You're not even going to think about it?'

'No.'

'Come on! It's been ages since you –'

'No,' Evie looks at Alex. 'Okay?'

'Okay.'

'But you can borrow my blue beaded cardi. It looks much better on you.'

'Thanks. Sorry if I was –'

'Forget it, Al.'

As Mr Powell makes his way to their desk, Evie feels her throat tighten.

'How's it going, girls?' he asks, looking straight at her.

'I think I'll start practising a front view.'

Slowly he nods. 'Okay.' He has said nothing about Evie resuming her portrait study. 'There's interesting light and tone from Alex's cheekbones. I'd work with charcoal first.'

Mr Powell takes a step, stops and turns back. 'I want you to write out your ideas for the series, Evie. This time, I want to know exactly what you're doing. Comprendo?'

'Yes, sir.'

As he walks away Evie leans over to Alex, pretending she hasn't felt the weight of his words. 'Do you think his jeans could be tighter?'

'Well, you've got to admit, he has got a cute bum.'

Evie slaps Alex. She squeals and Powell spins around, striding back to their desk.

'Is there a problem?' He directs the question to Evie.

'No, sir.' Evie's skin burns.

'Good,' he nods, his eyes fixed on her face. 'I'm sure you'd agree you've wasted enough time this year?'

He walks away.

'Bastard,' Alex whispers.

'Hmm?'

On the bus home Evie stares out the window, replaying his words in her head. Why did he have to remind everyone? is all she can think. It's invaded her headspace, leaving little room for any other thoughts.

'Dickhead,' she mutters. 'Dickhead, dickhead.'

Evie senses Powell's dislike of her. After 'the episode' – that's what the school counsellor called it – Powell told her mother he thought she was an attention seeker. But Evie knows the truth. He's in trouble – in trouble for not being aware of what was going on in his class that day. And for that, he'll never forgive her.

As the school bus reaches a corner known as 'the pin', Evie turns her head away. It is a habit or, as Evie feels, a necessity. She hates seeing the little girl standing at the corner. What does she want? Why is she still there after all these years?

Evie remembers sitting in the back seat of her parents station wagon. She is four years old. As they approach 'the pin' she sees the girl for the first time.

'Stop, Mummy,' she screams.

Her mother slams on the brakes and Evie jerks forwards in her seatbelt.

'Look, Mummy, look, Mummy. That girl. She's got blood on her. She's hurt herself.'

'Where? Where?' Her mother is opening the car door.

'There. Right there.'

Evie remembers pointing so hard her hand ached and she remembers her mother's head frantically twisting around trying to find the girl.

Rubbing her hand as if it still aches like it did that day, Evie sneaks a look out the bus window. She's not there.

'Hi, Evie.'

She hears the familiar voice. That's the other thing about 'the pin'. It's where the Wolsley College boys get on the bus and that means Seb Granger. Evie and Seb were at preschool together and had a kindy wedding. Her dad still teases her about it.

'This seat free?' he asks.

Seb's always keen for a chat. Usually Poppy is Evie's Seb repellant but she's away.

'Are they giving you heaps of work?' he asks, sitting down, shoving his double bass between them so she can only see the tip of his nose.

'Yeah.'

'Me too.' He attempts to stretch his long neck around the double bass case. Evie can't help giggling.

'I thought Year 11 was going to be a bludge, hey? But no way, man, they're already treating us like we're in Year 12. Maybe that's 'cause I'm at a private school but you're at a selective school, isn't that meant to be worse?'

'Maybe.'

'I've got two assignments and an essay to do by next week. Can you believe that? Slave labour, I reckon. Don't they know we actually have a life?'

'No.'

'You going to Taylor's party? It's going to be huge.'

As he craps on, Evie counts the stops till she's in a Seb-free enviroment.

She likes him, he wouldn't hurt her. But when he raves on and on she wishes the seat would swallow her.

Evie leans over the double bass. 'Bye, Seb.'

'Oh? Oh bye, Evie. I'll see you tomorrow.'

Walking up the driveway to the house, she spots her mother's face disappear behind the curtain.

'Spying on me now?' she says slamming the door.

'Evie!'

'I'm going up to my room.'

'How was your day?'

'You mean, did I do anything weird?'

'Evie!'

'I'm going up to my room. I've got stacks of work.'

Evie gets out her sketchpad and sharpens her pencils. She has made a decision.

'I am going to draw the best portraits ever,' she says out loud. 'I am going to perfect every shadow, every line and curve of Alex's face. I will capture the essence of who she is. It will be undeniable. And then,' her voice trembles, 'I'll hand my work to Powell and there will be nothing he can say except "Wow!".'

She studies the face she drew in class. She knows she'll need Alex's help and Alex'll give it. Her support is one thing Evie can be sure of. They need each other.

She takes Alex's school photo out of her folder. It's an enlarged individual one and unlike most school photos, actually does her justice. The scar above Alex's lip is just visible, but Evie understands the residual damage. 'Bunny' is what they called Alex at primary school; some still do.

Evie remembers feeling her blows, each one like a fist in the guts. She will never call her that name. They cannot help what they are born with.

Evie studies the photo. Taking a deep breath, she runs her finger around the eyes and draws their shape. Her eyes flick from the photo to the paper as she sketches and rubs out the lines that are emerging. Her grip on the pencil is tight; every now and then she stops to shake her hand. She takes off her cardigan and opens the window. She gets an elastic and ties her hair in a ponytail. She walks around the room a few times, sits down at her desk again and rubs out some more detail. She puts the cardigan back on and closes the window. Turning on the desk lamp, she stares at the oblong shapes that are Alex's eyes. 'Pathetic,' she groans, tearing her sketch up.

Hiding her face in her hands, she wonders – am I ready for this?

'Dinner in five minutes,' her mother calls.

'Piss off,' she whispers.

As Evie plays with the torn bits of paper, fitting them together like a puzzle, the face of the little girl at 'the pin' creeps into her mind. It's her eyes. Their vacant stare, the way they look through Evie as if she were made of air. Her mouth smiles and yet blood trickles out of her ear. Evie remembers how the drops splash onto the little girl's shoulder, a crimson circle bleeding into her yellow T-shirt.

A few days after that first time, Evie sees her again. The whole left side of her shoulder is covered in blood. It's so hot and the T-shirt, now a rusty brown, sticks to the girl's skin.

'Mummy,' she shrieks and points. 'Mummy, Mummy, that girl. She's there again.'

Her mother pulls into the kerb and stops the car, her face pale as she screams and shouts at Evie.

'That's not funny. Do you hear, Evie? That's not funny. There's no one there. Do you understand? Stop it, now!'

'But she's –'

'Shut up! Do you hear? Shut up!'

Evie begins to cry. 'But, Mummy.'

'I never want to hear such things again.' Now her mother's face is almost purple and she is breathing hard and fast. 'You can't see anyone because there is no one there to see. I never, ever, ever want to hear this again.'

But they pass that corner every day. Sometimes she's there, sometimes she's not. Now Evie knows to turn her head away and say nothing.

'Evie!' Robin calls once more. 'Come down for dinner, please.'

Evie picks up the bits of paper and throws them in the bin.

She waits for Alex and Poppy outside the Glebe markets. This is her favourite place to hang out. She watches people bargain with the stallholders. She knows who's tight and who'll give a good price.

A man calls, his accent thick, 'Oranges, sweet and juicy.' The deep vibration of a didge echoes through the ground, and spices from the Indian samosa van waft past. Here, among the colour and racket, Evie can escape.

Today she's wearing a long tweed coat with a fur-trimmed collar. Vintage of course. This coat makes her feel special, gives her confidence. It helps her say the right things, or rather, not say stupid things, especially in front of Ben, the silversmith. When she sees him her mind goes blank and she cannot think of a thing to say. That's when Ben smiles at her. Evie loves his smile – it's crooked and cheeky.

Evie fiddles with the fur collar and plans what she'll say to him. How she'll stand and look at him while they talk. A whistle makes her heart jump, then land with a plop – it's Poppy.

'Girlfriend, you look gorgeous – as usual. Did you get that coat here?'

'Sorry, darl, I got it at a second-hand shop in the country.'

'Typical,' sighs Poppy. 'I'd kill for one like that.'

Evie wonders what Poppy would do with a fur-trimmed tweed coat. A green jumper, jeans and trainers are all she ever wears in winter.

'We could find a good coat for you here.'

'Maybe,' Poppy shrugs. 'Anyway, what's Alex looking for?'

'A beaded cardi.'

'Like yours?'

'I told her to keep mine. It looks better on her.'

'Bullshit, Evie. Everything looks better on you. So when are we going to get our hands on silver boy?'

'You girls had better behave or I'll kill you.'

'There's Alex.'

Alex is wearing a felt hat, sunglasses, big earrings, a choker, a singlet and a man's coat with mega hipster pants. Poppy groans, Evie ignores.

'Cool coat, Evie.'

'Thanks. I love your earrings.'

'Really?' Alex fingers the beads.

'Yeah,' answers Evie. 'They're – exotic.'

'That's me, baby.' Alex wiggles her hips. 'Now, where's the Ben?'

'His stall's around the side.'

'Let's go.'

'Not yet,' Evie squeals. 'I'm too nervous. Oh god, can we have a wander around first?'

'Well, take us to the lady you get your great stuff from, I've never met her.' Alex links her arm through Evie's. 'That's if it's not a secret.'

'What do you reckon?' Evie turns them around. 'You coming, Poppy? Follow me, girlfriends.'

Evie holds her head high as she smiles and waves to the stallholders. Even with her eyes closed she could find her way to her favourite one just by following the scent of camphor and mothballs. She senses the stories mixed in their fragrance. Sometimes she thinks she hears them muffled and whispering like a badly tuned radio.

'And here,' she announces. 'Are the best vintage clothes ever.'

'Coming from the vintage queen, that's a big call.' Alex puts her hat on Evie's head.

They follow her through a maze of racks that bend in the middle.

'Wow,' the girls echo.

'Where do we start?' squeals Alex.

'Look at this,' Poppy calls. She holds up a fluoro orange jumpsuit with flared legs and a gold buckle.

'It's you, babe,' says Evie.

'It's thirty-five dollars!'

'Too expensive.'

'As if.'

'Hello, darlinks,' purrs Alex, emerging from behind a rack, wearing a full-length fur coat.

'Oh my god!' screams Poppy.

'You're not buying that, are you?' says Evie.

'Maybe? Do you like it, darlink?'

'Think of all the poor animals who died for that.'

'Keep your hat on, Evie.'

'Ha ha.'

'Hi, girls.' The woman's bangles jingle as she waves at Evie. 'Do you need help? Or is Miss Evie looking after you?'

'Hi, Petrina. These are my friends I was telling you about. This is Poppy and the politically incorrect one in the fur is Alex.'

'Hi,' they nod. 'Great stuff.'

'Thanks. I've been collecting for years. Have a good fossick around. Evie knows where I keep the good stuff.'

Petrina is one of those women whose age you can never guess. Her clothes are outrageously fantastic, that's a fact, but there are times Evie thinks she could be as old as fifty and as young as twenty. The one thing Evie does know about Petrina is there's an emptiness in her. When she's near her she feels it. It's like a cold breeze whistling through her chest and blowing out her spine.

'Check this, Evie.' Poppy holds up a Chinese satin opera coat that has a heavily beaded collar and cuffs.

'Wow. Try it on, Pop.'

Poppy slips her arms into the coat.

'Hello, sweetie,' she says in a posh accent. 'Would you like to come to the opera? I have two tickets for *Madame Butterfly*.'

Evie tries to laugh.

Alex leaps out from behind a rack of army coats, wearing a striped poncho, and a sombrero on her head. 'Buenas días, amigas!' she sings.

It makes Evie jump. She spins around wishing the girls would stop.

'My name is Hosé.' Alex continues. 'And I am from Mehiho.'

'Bravo.' Petrina claps as she watches their show. 'And who are you, Evie?' she calls.

But a low hum has started to vibrate in Evie's head. She's heard this noise before and it frightens her. It makes her want to crawl into a hole, be anywhere but here with the girls playing this game.

'Well, hello, Hosé,' Poppy chimes. 'My name's Daphne and I'm from London, darling.'

As the girls continue with their game Evie watches her hand, as though it were someone else's, reach out and pick up a shawl embroidered with hot-pink roses. Throwing it over her shoulders, she quivers as the silk lands gently on her skin. There's a musky perfume mixed with cigars and a deep smoky laugh, music and clapping. Her head tosses back and a voice emerges, 'I am a showgirl from South Africa. And my name is Jacqueline.'

Her trance is broken with their stare. Evie sees the creases forming on Petrina's forehead. Poppy has her hand over her mouth and Alex is pale. She realises what she has done. The horror encloses around her body.

'That's amazing,' gasps Petrina.

The shawl slips off Evie's shoulders. She grabs her coat and runs.

'Evie?' she hears Alex call.

Evie runs through the market, her coat dragging behind in the dirt. She keeps her head down as she weaves her way through the crowd, around the stalls and past silver boy. She keeps running until she reaches the main road. Cars toot as she swerves around the traffic. Her senses are raw and she can hear everything: a couple arguing over what brand of washing machine they're buying, a baby screaming in a café, a man singing opera in his bathroom. There is noise everywhere and she cannot turn it off.

She reaches the park on the other side and heads for a tree. It's offering her shelter. There she huddles under the branches and buries her head in her knees, her heart pulsating in her throat. She swallows hard, trying to force it back to its right place, but she knows now it will be hours before her throat relaxes and allows the saliva to slip gently down. She has felt this before.

The Moreton Bay fig towers above her making her feel so small, so pathetic, so out of control. She rubs her shoe on the twisted roots that have broken through the earth. Maybe she has always been like this? She wishes she knew, wishes someone could tell her.

She sees Alex and Poppy cross the road into the park. When they spot her they wave and start jogging. Evie bites her lip and waits for them. Puffing, they sit on either side of her. Alex puts her arm around Evie's shoulder. Evie tries not to flinch.

'You okay?'

'Not sure.'

Silence. She can't look at them. Not yet.

'God, you guys must think I'm weird.'

'Of course we don't,' replies Alex. 'We just don't want you to feel bad about . . . it.'

'Petrina must think I'm crazy. I'll never be able to face her again.'

'Don't be silly.'

'Did she say anything?'

Evie thinks she sees the girls exchange a look. She's not sure – perhaps it's her paranoia that creeps.

'She didn't say anything.'

'Promise, Alex?'

'She didn't, Evie,' adds Poppy.

'Honest?'

'Honest,' they say together.

The girls sit there for a while, not saying much.

'Are you still going to stay over?' Alex asks.

'I'm not sure.'

'Come on. Pretty please?' Alex sticks her nose in the air. 'I'll do my best profile poses.'

Evie manages a noise a bit like a laugh. 'You didn't get to meet silver boy.'

'We saw him for a second,' Poppy says. 'Alex told him we were friends of yours.'

'Oh my god,' Evie groans. 'What did he say?'

'Nothing. He just smiled.'

Through the chaos inside, Evie feels a smile try to lift the edges of her heart. My silver boy, she thinks. If only things could be that simple.

The three girls link arms and walk towards the road. Evie looks back at the Moreton Bay fig and envies its silence.

They cruise around the city for a while, Alex and Poppy doing most of the talking. Occasionally Evie says something but only to hide the fact that she feels completely distracted, not to mention freaked out. She isn't really aware what they're talking about. It's just background noise. Evie's trapped in her head, caught up in the confusion of what happened at the markets. Wasn't it simply an innocent game of dress ups? A bit of silliness? Is there anything she's able to do without being reminded of – it?

'What do you want to see?' says Alex.

Evie finds herself standing outside a cinema. She has no

idea that's where they were going. She has merely put one foot in front of the other.

'Are you sure you're okay to see a movie? You've been a bit, you know, quiet.'

'Yes, I'm sure,' lies Evie.

'How about *Miss American Pie*. It's on in fifteen minutes,' Poppy says, lighting a ciggie.

'What time is it?' Alex asks, taking Poppy's wrist. 'Nearly three.'

God, thinks Evie, where have I been for the last two hours?

'I'm starving,' she says, fanning the smoke out of her face. It's making her empty tummy feel sicker.

'I reckon we've got time to bolt down to Maccas,' says Alex.

'Okay,' they agree.

As long as Evie doesn't have to make any decisions, she'll be all right. At least Alex and Poppy will think she is.

Evie stares at the screen. She will not be caught out. When she hears laughter, she laughs; music, she taps her foot. She mobilises every brain cell in order to follow the plot and by the end of the movie she has a headache. But she is the first to say, 'That was great.'

She digests the looks of her friends.

'You reckon?' says Alex. 'I thought it was pathetic.'

'It was a bit stupid,' agrees Poppy.

'Well, I liked it,' Evie insists.

Evie goes to Alex's for a sleepover. They eat takeaway Vietnamese with Alex's mum. The brats are staying at their father's place, so it's not the nut house it usually is. Evie loves this place, all the more for the brat brothers and their shouting, the wrestling and thumping, the banging on doors and swearing and farting, skateboarding down stairs and bike racing through the hall, not to mention the endless burping competitions. Here Evie can escape. Here she isn't the only child, the carefully watched precious possession. Living here, she could just disappear.

With her mouth full Alex raves on about the brilliance of her new camera, then falls off the chair in a frenzy over the idea of schoolies week at the end of next year. Her mum, always working on the improvement of her daughter's appearance, launches into one of her speeches listing the reasons why Alex shouldn't have her hair cut and should have her eyebrows tidied.

'Bushy is in, Mum,' Alex keeps saying. 'Bushy's in.'

Evie knows this scene so well. She sits back listening to them, the lump in her throat dissolving.

'Shall we start?' Alex says, shoving the takeaway containers into the bin.

'Hey, aren't they recyclable?' Evie says.

'Probably.'

'You know they are. Don't just shove them in the bin.'

'Sowwy,' laughs Alex. 'I forget what a sensitive greenie you are.'

'They don't call me Evie Suzuki for nothing.'

'Well, I was the one to try on the fur coat.'

'I used to have a fur coat,' Alex's mum says. 'It was made of kangaroo.'

'Mum, you should have seen the stuff at the markets. Evie took us to the best second-hand –'

Evie interrupts 'I'm going to sharpen my pencils.'

She shuts the door to Alex's room. Posters of tanned, good-looking boys smirk at her. Evie tries to ignore them as she opens her art folder. Her hands shake when she sharpens the pencils. She puts them down and takes three deep breaths. Maybe she's not that relaxed, maybe the remnants of paranoia still lurk. She's not sure she can get through this but as the doorhandle turns, she fixes a smile on her face.

'Say cheese.'

Evie blinks as the flash goes off.

'You didn't say cheese.'

'You didn't tell me you were going to take my picture.'

'Where do you want me, darlink?' Alex drapes herself over the bed, rolls of flesh bulging over her hipsters.

'On the chair, thanks, darlink.'

'Say cheese.' Alex takes another photograph.

'What's your major work? Photographing unsuspecting victims?'

'This is an awesome camera and you're a good subject, girlfriend,' Alex informs her. 'I'm sure you could be a model, if you wanted to.'

'Exactly, if I wanted to. Now sit down and be quiet, muse.'

Alex sits on the chair. Evie tips her chin up and turns her face right then left.

'Don't move,' she says, walking back to her seat. She starts to sketch. The angle of Alex's face is perfectly positioned in this light.

'You're just like the text book says.'

'How?'

'Shh,' Evie says. 'Don't move.'

Alex sighs.

'I said don't move.'

'I didn't.'

'Your chest moved.'

'Pardon moi.'

'Shh.'

Evie likes the shape appearing on the paper. She needs this outline to work on.

'Can I move yet?' Alex whines.

'Two secs, I'm nearly finished.'

'What? The whole thing?'

'No, just the shape of your head.'

'Is that all? What about the rest of me?'

'I'll work on your features later.'

'I thought that's what you were doing in class yesterday?'

'I know, but my left eye kept watering and going fuzzy.'

'Oh?'

'It was annoying.'

'What was wrong with it?'

'I don't know. I probably had something in it.'

'Like an eyeball?'

'Funny.'

'Imagine if you have to get glasses.'

'That'd be okay.'

'You'd probably wear those funny old granny ones.'

'Shut up.'

'My dad had a friend with a glass eye. He used to wear a cat's eye.'

Evie shivers. 'That gives me the creeps. Let's change the subject.'

The rest of the weekend is uneventful, and on Monday morning Evie runs down the stairs two at a time. Second period is art and she's keen to show Powell the work she's done. To be honest, she'd like to shove the drawing up his arse, but she knows under the circumstances it would be unwise.

'Morning, Dad.' Evie kisses him as she does up the buttons of her cardigan. 'Hi, Mum.'

Robin doesn't look up from the toaster. Perhaps her parents have had another fight.

In Evie's world the walls are thin. Two nights ago she heard her mother hiss, 'Do I have to watch her every move?'

'She can't help it, Robin.'

'That's what you always say, Nick. You indulging her every second doesn't help either.'

The bedroom door opened. Footsteps down the stairs. The doona on the couch in the morning.

'Wow,' says Nick. 'I just had a flashback.'

Evie's mother groans as she butters the toast.

'What, Dad?'

'Do you remember when you were a little girl you used to have an imaginary friend?'

'Kind of.'

'You must have been about three or four. I know we were living in the old Annandale flat.'

Evie pours herself a cup of tea.

'What was my friend called?'

'Thena.'

'Thena?' Evie laughs. 'Did I have a lisp?'

'We used to hear you prattling on to her. Remember that, Rob?'

Evie's mother grunts.

'Anyway, you used to tell us she wore a red cardigan. That's what reminded me,' he says pointing to his daughter in her red cardigan. 'Except your friend's cardigan–'

'Thena, you mean,' corrects Evie.

'Yes, Thena. Pardon me,' he laughs. 'Anyway, you used to tell us that the buttons on Thena's cardigan were little blue teddies.'

'How tragic. I must have been desperate for a red cardigan with blue teddy buttons. God, Dad, don't tell Alex. She's the fashion faux pas queen, not me.'

'Your grandmother's friend knitted you one,' Robin says, joining them at the table. 'But then your father's mother loved to indulge your little fantasies.'

Evie watches her mother's stare sour her dad's reminiscence.

'Robin?' he mutters.

'What, Nick?' she replies, her eyes still fixed on his.

'See you later,' Evie says, taking her mug to the sink.

Evie needs no reminding that her mother hated her father's

mother. And these days Evie wonders is it for the same reason she can't accept her own daughter?

When Evie opens the door to the art room, she feels its innocence and happiness like red and yellow laser beams bouncing off the walls. That energy, full of optimism and hope, is what helped her return to school. She knows no one else sees it so she'll never tell anyone, not even Alex.

Alex is chatting to Antonia Cipri. Antonia is the new girl from the beginning of the year. She always sits at the front of the art room, except if Evie sits there. Evie and Antonia have hardly spoken and yet they already know too much about each other. Evie understands it's better to avoid her. It's like an unwritten law of social etiquette. Antonia blatantly avoids Evie and Evie still feels the shame.

'Hi, Evie,' Alex says, blushing.

'Hi.'

'Antonia was just telling me the video store's closing down.'

'Really?'

'You're not pissed off because I –'

'Of course not,' Evie says. 'It's a free world, Alex.'

'Sure?'

'Hey, remind me to give you the blue cardi. Taylor's party is this weekend, isn't it?'

'Have you changed your mind?'

'No way. I'm doing something with my dad.'

Evie prefers not to lie but sometimes it's a self-preservation policy.

Powell raves on about the Renaissance period, as if it were something he was personally responsible for. His voice grows louder with each new slide, and at one point his arms wave around so much he disconnects the remote control from the projector.

Evie stares at the slides, thinking how the women look a bit like Antonia. Thick hair, pale skin, big boobs, a large bum and super rosy cheeks. Evie tries not to think about that day. How the colour drained from Antonia's cheeks and the way she screamed and cried. It still makes Evie want to throw up.

She wraps her cardigan tightly around her chest and the slides begin to blur. Her left eye waters. She rubs it, making it worse, and for a second can't see out of it at all. She blinks hard and gradually the slides fall back into focus.

A practical session follows art theory. Evie lays out her work on the desk. She smooths down the edges of the paper, careful not to smudge the lines, and waits for Powell as he does his rounds. He always starts at one desk, working around the room in the same order. Evie wonders why he never varies this routine. He's the sort of teacher that loves to catch you out. Evie smiles at his missed opportunities. She will watch him every class, just in case. She will not be caught out. Not again.

Powell studies Evie's drawing. He walks behind her desk, moves to the left and then to the right. He even takes an upside-down view. Evie holds her breath.

'Not bad, considering.' And he moves to the next student.

She stares at the funny-looking clay figures belonging to the Year 7s. They are lined up, lopsided and quiet, waiting their turn to be fired and glazed. Evie knows she has to become like them: patient.

A ll week, Evie works hard on her drawings. The first completed portrait is due in two weeks. But drawing Alex's eyes is tricky. No matter what changes she makes, Evie cannot capture Alex's true expression. She knows handing it in even a day late will bring unwanted attention and she's determined to show everyone that she can pick up a pencil or piece of charcoal and draw again. No worries, no fears. If she can act like nothing happened maybe others can, too.

'You're working hard on your portraits,' Nick says one night, as they stack the dishwasher.

'Evie, don't scrape the plates like that.'

'Sorry, Mum.'

'Yes,' adds Robin. 'You have been spending a hell of a lot of time in your room.'

Evie doesn't reply. Instead she thinks about the clay figures.

'I'd like to see your portraits, too.'

'They're not quite finished, Mum.'

'Well, I can wait,' she replies. 'I'm good at that.'

Evie absorbs those words, knowing her mother still waits. Waits for her daughter to be different. Different, meaning the same. The same as everyone else's daughters.

'I'm just pleased you're drawing again, darling,' Nick says. 'I'd love to be able to draw. You're lucky – you inherited your mother's talent as well as her good looks.'

Robin clears her throat. Evie excuses herself and goes up to her room.

She isn't sure if she actually hears her mother say 'that's all she inherited from me', or whether she intercepts her mother's thought. She's become so accomplished at blocking thoughts that there are still times she finds it hard to differentiate a thought from real speech. The lessons have been hard and Evie knows it's better to keep quiet.

As a little girl, Evie always answers her mother, thinking it's the right thing to do. She doesn't understand it's a special thing, to hear a person's thought. She thinks she's the same as everyone else. No one bothers to tell her otherwise.

'They're next to the front door,' she calls to her mother one day.

'What's that?' her mother replies, looking under the couch.

'Your sandshoes.'

'My sandshoes? I can't find them anywhere.'

'They're at the front door.'

'Are they?'

Her mother walks to the front door.

'So they are. Thank you, my darling.'

'Don't put them on,' warns Evie.

Her mother snorts.

'I'm not a smartypants,' Evie says.

'I didn't say you were.'

'Yes, you did.'

'No, I didn't.'

'You did. I heard you.'

'I didn't say a thing,' her mother snaps. She's loosening the laces and stuffing her foot in.

'There's a b-b . . .' Evie whispers.

'Aaagghh,' her mother screams, ripping off the sandshoe.

In her head, Evie can see the bee. It's stuck in the toe part of the shoe, lying on its back, twitching.

'Did you put that in there?' her mother shouts.

'No, no. I promise, Mummy.'

'Well, how did it get there. How did you –'

'No, Mummy. I promise.'

Her mother hops around the doorway, holding her stung foot. She is crying.

'Mummy, I'm sorry. I saw it –'

'You can't, you can't.'

She limps away to the bathroom. Evie follows but her mother closes the bathroom door and locks it. Evie can hear her mother crying.

'Are you okay, Mummy?'

'Leave me alone, Evie.'

It's not until evening, when her father returns from work, that Evie's mother unlocks the bathroom door. It's never mentioned again.

In the safety of her room, Evie opens the drawing of Alex's face. She knows she has already given it too much time. She still has a history essay and a poetry assignment to complete. But she cannot concentrate on anything else.

'What's so special about your eyes?' she says, distracting herself from a low, monotonous hum that has started in her head. Sometimes if she ignores it, it goes away. 'Maybe it's your pupils.'

She rubs out the black dots in Alex's eyes and again colours in a new shape.

'There,' she puts down her pencil. 'An eyeball's an eyeball. Get over it, Evie.'

Balancing the portrait on the windowsill, Evie takes five steps back. The right eye is good. It's alive – it looks at Evie like Alex does. It makes the same connection. The left eye stares through Evie.

'Yuck,' she whispers. 'Don't look at me like that.'

Evie walks around her bed feeling the left eye follow her. Quickly she spins around as if to catch it out but its focus is still fixed on her. Now the hum is growing louder like it's travelled out of her head and into the room.

Evie sits on her bed, watching the black dot watch her. She stares till her eyes water and the face blurs and disappears. She blinks, pulling the picture back into focus, and a face stares back at her. It's not Alex. It's not the face she drew. It's a horrible face. Ugly, contorted, pleading.

Evie grabs her cardigan and throws it at the window, knocking the picture to the floor. She runs to the bathroom and locks the door.

'No. Please, no.' She slides down the tiled wall, gripping her throat.

'No, no, no,' she cries, thumping her fist on her thigh and

banging her heel on the hard floor. 'What do you want? Can't you just leave me alone?'

She sits there detached from any sense of time, every nerve in her body struggling to erase the face from her mind.

'Go, go,' she commands, rubbing the tips of her fingers across her forehead. 'Please go? Please? Don't do this again. I can't help you.'

'Evie?' her father's voice sounds like it's echoing through the door.

'Y-yeah?' Evie hears her bones crack as she struggles to her feet. Her backside tingles with the flow of fresh blood. 'I'm nearly finished.'

'You've been in there a hell of a long time.' He hesitates. 'Are you sure you're okay?'

Evie's hand supports her back as she leans over and flushes the toilet.

'I'm fine. I'll be out in a sec.'

'Well, goodnight,' he says. 'I'm off to bed.'

'Night.'

She looks at her watch. It's nearly eleven. How has she let time escape her control again? She washes her face and stares in the mirror. The whites of her eyes are bloodstained and her pupils expanded into the blue. She smiles at her reflection and it smiles back. She strokes her cheek and the girl in the mirror does the same.

'It's me,' she says, touching the mirror. 'Yes, it's definitely me.'

That night, Evie dreams of a young woman, a little older than herself. The girl stands with her back to Evie. Her dark copper-red hair hangs to her waist. It is matted at the crown of her head. She holds up her hand to show a ruby ring in the shape of a heart. A rumbling sound in the distance grows louder. It bursts into Evie's dream, all bells and thundering. The girl turns around. It is the same face as the one in the portrait. The girl reaches out her hand and tries to grab the sleeve of Evie's cardigan. Evie wants to help, she knows it's the right thing to do, it's what she's here for – but the pain and dread surrounding the girl are too much. Evie tries to pull her sleeve from the girl's grip. The girl holds on, stretching the sleeve towards her. Evie struggles to free her arms from the cardigan, then she runs. She turns back to see the girl doing up the cardigan. It is then she notices the buttons: they are little blue teddies.

'It's mine,' the girl whispers.

Evie opens her eyes and stares at the ceiling. She turns on the lamp and looks around the room. The furniture is in the same place and the blind is still down. She rolls up the sleeve of her pyjamas and runs her hand along her arm. It feels soft and warm. She smells her skin; the scent is hers. She looks in the mirror. The side of her face is creased from the blanket and her eyes are small, like they should be after sleep.

'It's still me,' she whispers.

Evie plays her Jeff Buckley CD softly.

'Fall in light, fall in light. Feel no shame for what you are. Feel no shame for what you are.'

When she loses control and the darkness stalks her she feels as though these words were meant for her.

'Fall in light, grow in light.'

Evie holds up her hand, her long fingers curling in the shadows.

'Don't belong. Don't belong. You and the stars. Throwing light . . . Fall in light, fall in light . . .'

Evie opens her mouth, catching a tear that runs down her face.

'Don't belong. Don't belong,' she whispers.

'Here we are.' Evie hands Alex the blue beaded cardigan.

'Thanks.' Alex hugs her. 'I wish everything was, you know, normal and that you would come to the party.'

'How can I?'

Alex plays with her fingers. 'Is it going to be like this forever?'

'Like how?'

'Like you never going out – because of what happened?'

'I don't know.'

'It sucks.'

'I can't help it, Alex.'

'I know. The whole thing is such a shit.'

Evie nods.

'I mean, I don't mean what you do or that sort of stuff. You can't help it. I know that. It's just everyone else, they're so, so – pathetic the way they can't handle what happened.'

'Alex, my mum can't even handle it. She thinks I'm a freak.'

Evie sees Antonia Cipri walk up to the library. Her steps are slow and cumbersome.

'It's not like I had that many friends before,' Evie says. 'You and Poppy have always been my real friends. It's not like I lost anything.'

'It doesn't matter,' sighs Alex. 'It still sucks what they did.'

Evie shrugs.

'I'd love to know who did it,' hisses Alex.

'Why? It wouldn't change anything.'

They watch Antonia return from the library.

'Do you think it was her?' asks Alex.

'Definitely not,' Evie answers. 'She's not like that. You know, she's so sad. I think I felt sorry for her, even before.'

'She seems to be on a permanent downer. Not, not, 'cause of –'

'Yeah, I know,' Evie sighs. 'She's hardly been at school this term.'

'I hadn't noticed.'

How fortunate, Evie thinks. She will always be aware of Antonia.

'Maybe I won't go to Taylor's party, as a protest.'

'As if! You've never missed a party in your life. Remember you insisted on going to Tom Kessler's ninth birthday even though you had the chickenpox?'

'Yes,' laughs Alex. 'I was so itchy. Remember, I had one in my –'

'Yes, I remember!'

'That was awful.'

'Go and have a rage, love. Just promise one thing?'

'What?'

'Give us all the goss. Okay?'

'Cross my heart.'

On Saturday morning, Evie gets up early. She washes her hair, shaves her legs and after trying on seven different outfits, settles for the faded jeans, a dusty pink petticoat she found at an antique store, Blundstones and a double-breasted pea-coat from an army disposal shop. She wants to look good but she's not prepared to freeze. She twists her hair in a low bun, ties a fine piece of leather string around her neck and puts on some lip gloss. She smiles at her reflection saying, 'Hi, Ben. I'm sorry I had to rush off last time. I, um . . .'

She decides not to mention it.

Nick looks up from his newspaper. 'Where are you off to looking so gorgeous?'

'You'll freeze,' butts in Robin.

'I have a coat, Mum.'

'You're not taking that shabby old coat, are you?'

'Clay figures, clay figures,' Evie whispers.

'What happened to that lovely navy woollen jacket I bought you?'

'Ummm?'

'You never wear anything I buy you. It was so expensive and I –'

'Well, I'm off to the markets.' Evie cuts her mother's impending lecture.

'Do you want a lift?' Nick asks.

'Only if you're going up the street, Dad.'

'Rob, let's go and have a coffee.'

'Nick, I have to catch a plane in two hours and I have twenty-seven essays to mark.'

'Come on, hon. We've got time.'

'Nick, if you want to take Evie to the markets, take her. But I don't have to go too.'

'I thought it'd be nice to have a coffee together before you go away.'

'Dad, I'll get the bus.'

'There we are, Nick. She says she'll get the bus.'

'Well, I'd like to take her.'

'Nick, you can't protect her forever.'

He stands there staring at her. 'I just offered her a bloody lift, Robin.'

Evie waves and closes the door. 'Bye.'

'Hang on,' her dad calls.

He stops the car at the footpath. 'Get in.'

Evie climbs into the front seat. 'Sorry, Dad,' she says. 'Are you guys okay? I feel so bad that it's –'

'It's not your fault. She can't help it.'

'Can't help what? Hating me?'

'Evie, she's your mother, for godsake. She loves you.'

'Dad, that's such a typical parent thing to say.'

'Well, it's true. Of course she loves you. You're her daughter.'

'Just not the daughter she wanted,' Evie says, staring out the window.

'That's not true. It means so much to her being a mother, having a daughter. I think it's something she craved all her life.'

'Why do you say that?'

'She was so little when her mother died, Evie. She was brought up by a string of housekeepers. Sometimes five or six different ones in a year.'

'What about her father?'

'Well, he was hardly the warmest man in the world.'

'See, she can be like that too.'

'She tries.'

'Look, Dad, you know what I'm saying.' Evie turns to face him. 'Ever since that stuff happened at school and mum's been seeing a counsellor, she's been so – so cut off. At least she used to try and pretend I wasn't a freak. Now she can't even do that.'

'She was the same with my mother,' he says.

'Well, what's it going to take? Me predicting an earth-quake or something?'

'Evie, it hasn't been easy for her. At least I know about this. I mean, I grew up with it around me. People were always coming to the house to see my mum. "Is Anna here? I need Anna to read for me." At all hours of the day and night.'

'Did it bother you?'

'No. That's what I'm trying to say. To me, it was completely normal. That's the way my mother was.'

'What about Grandpa? What did he think?'

'He thought she was special.' He pauses. 'She was special.'

'I wish Mum could think like that.'

'Look, she's trying. That's why she's seeing a counsellor. There are lots of things she has to work through. Her father wasn't at all tolerant of, let's say, supernatural things. He was a minister and more than that he was a very harsh man.'

'Did he like you?'

'Not much but then he didn't like anyone much and he especially didn't like my mother.'

'Sounds familiar.'

They drive the rest of the way in silence.

As Evie gets out of the car her dad calls, 'Evie? Here,' and hands her fifty dollars.

'Dad, it's okay.'

'Take it. Please? You're a good girl, Evie.'

She smiles. 'Thanks.'

A busker smiles at her as she walks through the market gates. Evie takes a deep breath and feels her heart flutter. She is nervous about seeing Ben, but then she always is. It's a 'good nervous', full of butterflies and secret smiles. It's facing Petrina she dreads. Not physically, it's just that she's never had to face it here. Here she has always been free, nameless. Simply a girl from somewhere who loves second-hand clothes. No reputation or rumour follows. The market has been like her refuge, her escape.

She goes to see Ben first but he's not at his stall. She looks around for him. Sometimes she pretends he'll walk up to her and say, 'Hey, babe, let's go and have a curry.' He'll buy her a mixed plate and they'll sit on the grass discussing Post-modernism and the French Impressionists. She's sure he's into all that. He looks arty and sophisticated.

'G'day.'

Evie looks up to see Ben's crooked smile. He holds a meat pie smeared with way too much tomato sauce.

'Ben? Hi.'

He takes a huge bite. 'So, are you all better?'

'Sorry?'

'Are you better?' he says with his mouth full. 'You were crook last time.'

'Huh?'

He spits out a bit of gristle. 'I saw you running for your life.'

'Oh?'

'I spoke to your friends. One of them said your guts were a bit off.'

'Oh?' She can't stop staring at the tomato sauce smeared over his chin.

'She said you were making a run for it.'

'Did she?'

'Had you eaten one of those curries?' Now flakes of pastry sit on the corners of his mouth.

'No.'

'Just as well.' He swallows the last bit.

'Yeah?'

'Well, I'd better get back.' He wipes his hands on his jeans. 'See you.'

'Yeah. See you.'

Evie buys herself a mixed plate at the Indian samosa van and sits on the grass. Scrambled thoughts swim in her head. She can't get his words or the image of him eating that pie out of her brain. 'Silver boy's a yobbo? Oh my god!' She lets a laugh escape. A kid stops and stares.

'Hello,' giggles Evie.

'What are you laughing at?' the kid asks.

'Nothing. Everything.'

'What's that?'

The kid is called away before Evie can answer. From the grass she can see Petrina folding brightly coloured mohair jumpers. She wears the poncho Alex wore that day. Evie gets up, throws her rubbish in the bin, clears her throat and walks over.

'Hello.'

'Evie!' Petrina gives her a hug. 'I wondered when you'd come back to see me. Hey,' she says, searching Evie's face, 'you're not embarrassed, are you?'

Evie shrugs. 'A bit.'

'Evie, you are so special.' Petrina holds her hand. 'I've always thought that and now I know why.'

Evie's hand feels limp in Petrina's. Petrina squeezes it and holds it firmly.

'If I could've had children,' for a moment she pauses. 'Well, no chance of that happening.'

Evie frowns.

'Long story.'

'Oh?'

'I was in an accident. No one's fault really,' is all Petrina says.

The same breeze whistles through Evie's chest and out her spine – Petrina's emptiness.

'Anyway, what I'm trying to say is I would've been proud to have had a daughter like you.' She lets Evie's hand go. 'So, I don't want you to think any more about it. Deal?'

Evie nods. 'Deal.'

Petrina pulls something out from under the table. 'This is for you.' She hands Evie a parcel wrapped in purple tissue paper.

'Oh my god.' Evie holds up the fringed shawl. The pink roses spill out of the fabric. 'Thank you.'

'It was my mother's Great-Aunt Jacqueline's,' Petrina's voice trembles. 'She was born in Johannesburg and she was a cabaret dancer.'

Evie feels her throat tighten. It always feels like this when she's forced to swallow who she is.

'Evie, I don't know anyone like you. I have no idea what it'd be like.'

'It can be scary,' Evie whispers.

Again, Petrina hugs her. Evie nestles her face in the soft wool of the poncho and breathes in the camphor and moth-balls.

At home, Evie wraps the shawl in its purple tissue paper and carefully places it in the bottom drawer of her wardrobe. This is where she keeps her most treasured pieces.

An original 1970s Fendi silk scarf, thigh-high green suede boots, a brown snakeskin handbag. Evie had hesitated before buying this, but decided there was nothing she could do about the inhumane things they did to animals back then. She has silk stockings still in their original packet and a pair of white Staggers denim flares. She knows high-waisted jeans will make a comeback some day.

Her favourite thing is a square-shaped bangle made of silver. It's from Russia and it was her grandmother's. Evie opens the lid of its box and runs her fingers along its smooth inner curve. She has never worn the bangle, her excuse being it's too valuable. This is true, but somewhere she knows the real reason. She senses its power – something left over from her grandmother. She knows there'll be a time when she's meant to wear it and sometimes she feels that time will be soon. Evie shuts the box, packs everything back in the drawer and closes the wardrobe.

It is six thirty. She thinks of Alex and Poppy getting ready for Taylor's party. She wonders what Alex will wear with the blue beaded cardigan. Alex's tendency to hit and miss – badly – in the dressing department makes Evie worry for her. She understands what people can be like. Protecting Alex is something she's good at.

Evie wonders who'll be there. Who'll get off with whom? Who'll get pissed and be a dickhead and who'll notice she isn't there? Her self-imposed exile seems to affect no one. But, Evie wonders, is it completely self-imposed? She has had help. Someone has let her know she isn't welcome in society. That people like her are not suited to general integration.

She closes her eyes and pictures the words that tell her this. The words that make sure she understands the rules. The ugly black letters are scrubbed and scrubbed off the school's toilet door but the message remains clear in Evie's head. As the day goes on, it is added to. The third toilet cubicle on the left becomes a kind of free-for-all – come and add your comment, a come and pass your judgement type of list.

Watch the Witch she's watching you.
I don't see dead people – I draw dead people.
BURN THE WITCH!
Evie Simmons is an evil bitch.
Evie Simmons is an EVIL WITCH.

Evie remembers walking towards the locker room. Her locker door is hanging open, lopsided on one hinge. Her bag is on the ground and all her things are spread across the floor. Her pencil case, tampons, hairbrush, a drink bottle. Her sketchbook is ripped down the middle and muddy shoe marks are smeared across her carefully drawn lines. She tries to place one foot in front of the other as she walks towards her locker door. She reaches out her hand and pushes the door closed. Painted on the door are a cross and the words 'SIC BITCH'. She hears her breath, a shallow gasping sound, as she tries to swallow the scene. She picks up her torn sketchbook; the paper rustles. She cannot stop her hand from shaking. There are tears – she recalls wiping them away with her sleeve. Someone is holding her hand.

It's Alex. She is leading her somewhere. She takes her into a room. Her parents are there. She cannot remember any more.

'Evie?' Nick calls. 'I'm going to get a video. Do you want to come too?'

Her dad's voice brings her back to her room. She lies on her bed, here in the present entrenched in the past.

'Hang on,' she calls. 'I'll come with you.'

They cruise around the shelves of the video store. She likes her dad's taste in movies. He has opened her up to the world of foreign films, especially the French comedies.

They meet up in the new releases section. Evie swallows hard as her eyes flick over the titles of videos she knows she will never watch, those her father will never suggest. She can trust him in that way, always. They agree on a British film about a woman who grows hydroponic dope to pay off her dead husband's debts.

'So you're spending another Saturday night with your old man?' he says on the way home.

'You're not that old,' Evie replies. 'Besides, what else am I going to do?'

'What are Alex and Poppy doing tonight?'

'Going to a party.'

'You didn't want to go?'

'It's just some guy from Year 11 at Wolsley College. No one interesting.'

'Is Seb going?'

'Seb? Probably. How should I know?'

'Just asking. How is your old kindy husband? Has his voice broken yet?'

'Dad, get over it!' Evie winds down the window and breathes in the evening smog. 'Anyway, I still haven't graduated from the leper colony.'

'Evie!'

'Well, I haven't. It's true and you know it. I've been back at school – what, nine weeks?'

'Ten.'

'I still feel everyone's eyes on me.'

'Are you sure you're not imagining it?'

'I wish.'

'Maybe we should talk again about you changing schools. That was what your mum wanted you to do.'

'For all the wrong reasons,' mutters Evie.

'There are other schools with good art departments. Schools that offer the same type of thing.'

'Oh, I don't know, Dad,' Evie sighs. 'It's not like I've been demoted from most popular girl or anything. I've always been a bit on the outer and I liked it that way. Now, I'm still on the outer but I'm wearing a big fluoro sign that flashes "weirdo".'

They stop at a red light and watch a man with a long, scruffy beard stumble across the road. Every couple of steps he takes a gulp from a brown paper bag.

'You know what's worse than being on the outer and no one noticing you?'

'No?' Nick replies.

'Being on the outer and everyone noticing you. It's so – so demeaning.'

'Evie, you're clever, talented, beautiful –'

'Stop it, Dad. I'm a freak. Maybe not to you but to everyone else I am.'

She feels the pang of her father's sigh. She turns to him and tries to smile.

Theo, her dad's best friend, also known as 'the aftershave king', comes over to watch the video with them. He's like an uncle to Evie. As boys, Nick and Theo delivered the local paper. As teenagers, they wrote for the school paper and dreamt of starting their own publication, *The Scoop*. Now they work together on Radio News.

They love to tell their stories, always the same ones. The doberman chasing them, interviewing the prime minister of Italy, and the time they ran a story on exam cheating techniques and were suspended from school for two weeks.

They crack Evie up, not so much the stories – she knows them off by heart – but the way they butt in and contradict one another like an old married couple. It's always the same, Theo convinced his version's right, Nick shaking his head saying, 'You know, Theo, I don't remember it like that.'

'Of course you don't.' Theo's reply never changes. 'You were too busy trying to please everyone.'

'Good night, Evie,' Theo says as he's leaving. 'Don't go getting any smart ideas from that movie, hey?'

'Unfortunately, Theo, as you know I don't need illegal substances to get my imagination going.'

He squeezes her shoulder. She gives him a quick peck, trying to suppress the giggles. His cologne really is over-powering tonight.

'See you, big girl.'

Evie and Nick sit in the kitchen drinking hot chocolate. Evie blows on her milk, watching the skin layer swirl around the top of the mug.

'Do you think Theo realises how much he stinks?'

'I think he thinks he smells beyouuudifool.'

'Yeah, he makes me laugh. Does his sister still read tea cups?'

'Coffee cups,' Nick corrects. 'That's another Greek thing. Ask Theo about it, they're all into it.'

'When's Mum back from Canberra?'

'Tomorrow night.'

'Is she staying at Paula's?'

'Where else! You could've gone with her, Evie. She would've liked that.'

'Nah. All they do is talk about the old days at art college. It gets boring.'

'Tell me about it.'

'Lucky ducks. I bet they'll go and see the Matisse exhibition.'

'How are your drawings coming along? I still haven't had the pleasure.'

'Okay,' she lies.

She loves talking to her dad when it's just the two of them. She feels like she can tell him anything – just not everything. If she tells him she is having trouble with the portraits, that the eyes follow her around the room, she knows his forehead will crease and he'll get that look on his face. It's like an injection at the doctor's – no matter how prepared you think you are it still hurts, a lot.

'Time for bed,' Nick says, looking at his watch.

'Me too.' She kisses him goodnight. 'Dad?'

'Yes, Evie?'

'That day, at school with Antonia and stuff?'

'Yes?'

'What did they say when they rang you?'

'They rang Robin, not me.'

'Well, what did they say to Mum?'

'Gosh, Evie.' He rubs his temples. 'I think they said there'd been an incident.'

'An incident?'

'Well, I think that's the word they used.'

She nods.

'Why, Evie?'

'Just wondering.'

She sits on the toilet, her head in her hands. She doesn't know why she asked her dad that. She knows it doesn't matter now. But for some reason she just wanted to know how they described it. What actual word they used.

If Evie stays very still and concentrates, she can hear Antonia's shrieks. Sometimes she can conjure up the entire scene in her head. It plays like a movie but in slow motion, with the sound echoing through her skull. Antonia's chair crashing to the ground. The look in Powell's eyes as he yells, white stuff foaming at the corners of his mouth. And a tightness around her neck, trapping the air.

Wednesday the 10th of April, Evie Simmons, a quiet girl from Year 11, walks into the art room. She walks out as someone else.

It's the second lesson in her elective subject of portrait drawing. She is keen and she is good at it. Powell walks around the room, explaining the various techniques used in drawing a face. The girls are taking notes. He tells them to study the facial features of the person they're sitting next to. He gets them to draw a head shaped like an egg and to then make a vertical centre line.

Evie sits next to Antonia Cipri, the new girl from Brisbane. Antonia seems shy as Evie studies her face, dividing it into sections on the page.

'How are you going?' Powell asks, standing over Evie.

'Good, I think.'

'It's a really good shape, Evie.'

'Thanks. Do I have time to try the whole face today?' asks Evie. 'I've been doing a lot of practice at home, from photos and stuff.'

Powell checks his watch. 'Sure. Give it a go. I like enthusiasm in my students.'

Evie smiles.

'Is that okay with you, Antonia?' he asks. 'Perhaps you can do Evie's face next week?'

Antonia blushes again.

'I'm good at sitting still,' she says to Evie.

And she is. Evie spends the double period drawing, rubbing out, shading then adding a bit more. Every now and then Antonia smiles. Evie can see Antonia's face in front of her and coming alive on the paper. The creation is exciting.

'Do you like doing portraits?' Antonia asks tucking her hair behind her ears.

'Wow, your ring!' Evie takes Antonia's hand and studies it. 'Is it old?'

'No.'

'It's beautiful. Can I try it on?'

Antonia hesitates. 'Ah –'

'It's okay.'

'No. No, you can. It's . . . it's my brother's.'

'Yeah? I thought it might've been a guy's ring. It's kind of chunky.' Evie admires it on her hand. 'I like it.'

'Thanks.'

'Looks better on you.' Evie says handing it back. 'Better get back to work. Powell's doing his rounds.'

'You're a really talented drawer, Evie. I've noticed your stuff.'

'Thanks.' Evie blushes this time. 'I hope you'll like this.'

'Give us a peep.'

'Hey?'

'Give us a look.'

'Not yet,' Evie snaps. She looks around. 'Sorry,' she

whispers. 'I don't – know where that came from. God, I'm really, really sorry, Antonia.'

Antonia mutters something.

Evie's eyes flick up to her face then back to the paper, as she tries to concentrate on the final features, but she's restless in her chair. A humming sound has started playing in her head, a drone monotonous yet menacing, and something is happening to the drawing. The picture doesn't seem right. Evie's foot is tapping the floor, louder and faster. Some of the girls are looking at her; she's sure they're whispering.

'Are you okay?' Antonia asks.

'I'm not sure.' Evie puts her hands on her forehead. Antonia leans over and takes the pad.

'Let me have –' she starts to say before the colour drains from her face.

Antonia turns white and starts to suck in air like she can't get a breath. The noise is loud. It's scaring Evie.

'Antonia?' Evie stands up. 'Antonia?'

'No,' Antonia whispers. 'No, no.'

She starts to scream. Her chair is knocked to the ground. She holds on to the desk, her body shaking. Powell catches her as her legs give way.

'Antonia, Antonia?' he is shouting. 'Can you hear me?'

The girls gather around.

Powell is shouting at Evie. 'What happened?'

Evie can't move, can't speak. She has just seen what Antonia has seen.

Antonia struggles out of Powell's hold and runs to the door.

It slams behind her. Silence follows and then in one synchronised move, one succinct sound, they all turn to look at Evie.

Powell now holds the sketchpad. White foam bubbles at the side of his mouth.

'What's this?' he's yelling. 'What's this?'

Evie turns her face. She cannot look at the drawing he is holding up in front of her. That and the noise in her head is confusing her: she doesn't understand how it got there. It isn't Antonia's face any more. It's the face of a young man. His eyes bulge out of his head and his lips are swollen. His tongue sticks out of his mouth and there is a mark on his neck. Evie throws up, bits of her insides splattering onto the young man's face.

Evie's mind resurfaces. She hates this memory but it will never leave her alone. She gets off the toilet and walks to the mirror. She studies the face that stares back and thinks of her friends at Taylor's party. Have they thought of her?

'Who am I?' she whispers. 'What am I?'

PART TWO

'All major work propositions due in today,' announces Powell. 'On my desk as you're leaving, please.'

Evie shuffles her papers, knocks her pencils off the table and leans down, picking them up one by one. From under there she checks the classroom has emptied. She can see Powell's grey-trousered legs standing by his desk. She gets up and walks towards him. He doesn't look up.

'On my desk, Evie.'

'I don't have it, sir.'

He clicks his tongue and goes to speak. She gets in first.

'It's just taking a little longer than I expected, sir.'

'I'm sure it's a good reason.' His sarcasm stings. 'Come on, I'm dying to know.'

He stands there, his silence forcing Evie to babble on. He loves a game, she thinks.

'Could I, I mean I know it's, well, what I really need is a week's extension.'

'You've got three days, Evie. I want it by Thursday. End of discussion.'

'Thank you, sir.' Perhaps I should get down and kiss his feet, she thinks. That'd spin him out. She settles for another 'thank you' and crawls out of the art room.

Alex is in the canteen queue.

'There you are,' Evie says.

'The brats raided the fridge before I got a chance to make my lunch,' Alex groans.

'No pushing in,' says one of the CGs from Year 12.

'I'm not buying anything,' Evie replies.

The girl mutters something. Alex spins around.

'What did you say?'

'Nothing.'

'Crap. I heard what you said.'

Evie shakes her head. 'Leave it, Al.'

'What a bitch.'

'Don't go there, Alex.'

'God, sometimes I really hate this place.'

Evie nods. She wonders what the girl said but asking Alex right here, in the canteen line, will only invite trouble. Evie could do without the attention.

'Those CGs think they rule. Anyway, more importantly, did you hand your major work proposal in?'

'No.'

Alex's jaw drops. 'Are you mad?'

'It's not finished.'

'It's not finished?'

'No.'

'But that's all you've been doing the past few weeks!'

'I know, I know.'

'So, what's the story, glory?'

'Alex, I desperately need your help.'

'How?'

'I need you to sit for me again. I can't finish the initial drawings with only your photo, it just isn't working and Powell won't –'

'Evie, I've got –'

'It's just for the next three days. The oldies will go spastic if they find out I haven't handed it in. Please, pretty please? I'll be your best friend.'

'You already are.'

'Be even better.'

'Well, I definitely can't do it on Wednesday, I've got hockey, and you'll have to come to my place tomorrow because I have to mind the brats.'

'What about this arvo? At my place?'

'Today? Yeah, should be okay.'

'Thank you. I owe you majorly, love.'

'I know, love.'

Evie waits while Alex orders at the counter.

'A ham and pineapple pizza pocket and a hot chocolate, please.'

Evie notices a canteen mother looking at her, a buttery knife poised in the air. Another mother whispers something in her ear. Evie knows it's the woman who insisted her mother resign from the art committee. 'It makes the school look bad,' she had said. They look at Evie like a couple of magpies, then nod in unison. The first mother goes back to buttering the sandwiches. The second mother stares for that extra second. Evie quickly looks away. She's been back at school twelve weeks and she knows now to expect this.

At first, Evie doesn't think the situation with Antonia is complicated. She wishes she could give an explanation, make it simple and straightforward; her mother would prefer that. But Evie doesn't understand what happened. So she'll pretend it was nothing, just like her mother pretends that the little girl at the pin was nothing.

Their first session with the school counsellor reveals the situation with Antonia is complicated, very complicated.

Evie sits on a chair facing the counsellor. Her parents sit behind her. She doesn't like not being able to see her mother's face. She has only her voice to guide her.

'Tell me about what happened, Evie,' the school counsellor almost whispers.

'I'm . . . I'm not really sure, Mrs O'Leary.'

'Please, call me Bernie.'

Evie nods and tries a smile.

'I didn't draw it on purpose. It just sort of happened.'

Bernie nods back, encouraging in her smile. Her top front tooth is grey and cracked.

'Had you spoken to Antonia much, before this, er, episode?'

'Not really. She's pretty shy, being new at the school.'

'Evie, did you know her brother had died?'

Silence.

'Evie?'

Evie squeezes her fingers. 'No,' she breathes.

'I'm telling you this because of what happened. But I want you to understand it's a very private and distressing matter for the Cipri family.' Bernie recrosses her legs. 'Antonia's brother hung himself in the park across the road from where they lived in Brisbane.'

She hears her father gasp. She turns around to him. He stands up and pushes his chair next to her.

'That's better,' Nick whispers and gestures back to his wife.

'I'm okay here,' she answers.

Evie is certain her mother's only just handling this.

Nick turns back to the counsellor. 'How old was he?' he asks.

'Eighteen,' replies Bernie, passing Evie a tissue.

'I'm so sorry,' Evie blurts through her tears. 'I didn't, I . . .'

Evie can't say anything else. Her throat is swollen and aches. All she can do is choke on the memory of that day.

'Evie, this is a very difficult situation.' Bernie is whispering again. 'My job is to help you not feel alone through this. And my job is also to reassure the students and parents that this was not – how do I say – intentional, on your part.'

Evie nods, it's hard to get a breath through the sobs.

'There are many people who don't know how to handle this sort of thing. They're shocked, probably a bit frightened. This situation is – unusual. We have to think about how people may react.'

'Of course,' begins Nick. 'Our concern is Evie and supporting her through this. Isn't it, Robin?'

But Robin says nothing.

Evie touches the back of her head. It suddenly feels hot. She presses her hand against the spot, trying to deflect her mother's stare.

'Thanks for this, Alex,' Evie says, as they walk home from the bus stop.

'It's okay. I know you'd do it for me. Hey, Seb was having a bit of a perve on you, I noticed,' teases Alex.

'Piss off, Alexandra.'

'He was.'

'So?'

'Poppy says he bashes everyone with his double bass trying to get a seat near you.'

'He likes a chat, that's all.'

'He was at Taylor's on Saturday night.'

'Lucky him.'

'Poppy and I reckon he was looking for you.'

'God, it must have been a boring party.'

'Poppy reckons she heard him say your name.'

'What were you guys doing? Stalking him?'

'Poppy said she walked past a group and heard him say "Evie" something or other.'

'Poppy – no, you're both sick in the head and in need of a life,' dismisses Evie. She has always considered Seb harmless, almost trustworthy.

They take a drink and a packet of biscuits up to Evie's room. Alex goes to the toilet. Evie gets her pad and pencils ready.

'Okay,' Alex returns. 'Where do you want me?'

'Um, over there,' Evie points. 'I'm just going to the loo, too.'

Evie washes her face and pulls her hair back into what she calls her drawing hairdo. 'I can do this,' she whispers. She takes three long, deep breaths and tries to push the horrible face out of her head. 'Just relax and draw.'

As she opens the door to her room a rush of panic floods her body. Alex is holding up the portrait in her sketchpad.

'Who's this ugly bitch?'

Evie lurches towards her. 'Don't!' she yells.

Alex squeals. 'What are you doing?'

She snatches the pad and sits down. She loudly flips the pages over, looking for a blank one. When she looks up, Alex is still standing there staring at her. Evie looks at Alex but can't think of anything to say. Her head is buzzing but her mind is blank.

'Say something, Evie!'

Evie shrugs and presses her lips together.

'Tell me what it is. Come on.'

Evie goes to speak but the sound is stuck somewhere between her throat and her mouth.

'Who is it in that drawing?'

Silence.

'Why didn't you want me to see it?'

Silence.

'Evie?'

Silence.

'Evie talk to me.'

'It started out as – you.'

'Me?'

Evie nods.

'But . . . but that's not one of the portraits of me?' Alex is talking fast. 'It doesn't look anything like me, even on a bad hair day. I mean, I know I'm not the most beautiful thing in –'

'I can't hand them in, Alex.'

'But I saw some of the drawings of me. They were fantastic. Well, as fantastic as they can be. They certainly weren't like that ugly scrag.'

'Alex, you don't understand. You never saw a finished one.'

'So? What's the diff? Where are those ones of me?'

'Shit, Alex,' Evie's voice cracks. 'Don't you get it?'

'Evie?' Alex puts her arms around her. 'You're shaking.'

'I've been feeling pretty freaked out.'

'How long? You should have told me.'

'I don't know what I'm going to do!' Evie's body feels so heavy. 'I don't want anyone to know about this. God, Mum and Dad, especially Mum, just won't handle it.'

'Handle what? Evie?'

Gently Alex holds her face but Evie turns away. It hurts everywhere.

'Evie? God! I know what you're saying now. This is like the Antonia thing, isn't it?'

'Yep.'

Alex drops her hands. 'Shit.'

For a while they sit there not speaking. Evie watches Alex stare out the window. She has to give her time to digest. It's a big ask, she knows.

'It's getting dark early,' Alex says.

'We've just had the shortest day of the year,' Evie tells her. 'The winter solstice.' She walks to the window. The trees have lost their leaves. How ugly and naked they look against the landscape. 'I read an article about it the other day. It's known as the dark half of the year.' She pulls the blinds down. 'It's true,' she whispers, sensing something awful yet not being exactly sure what.

Evie lies on her bed with just one thought: how can this

be happening again? Alex sits with her feet on the desk, turning the lamp on and off.

'Evie?'

'Yeah?'

'Can you tell me what happens with, with . . . the portraits?'

'I don't know, they just change. I mean, I'm the one holding the pencil, making the lines and shapes but somehow it doesn't turn out the way I'm seeing it. If you know what I mean? It's pretty weird to understand.'

'So it's exactly like what happened with Antonia?'

'Exactly.'

'So, you're like drawing a person that's sitting in front of you.'

'Yes, that I'm looking at. I mean their face is right there. Well, I was drawing with your photo but the face that ended up on the paper is a face I've never seen before.'

'Far out.'

'It's happened a few times now.'

'The same face?'

'Every time.'

'You could lie.'

'How do you mean?'

'You could tell Powell you decided not to draw me. You could pretend it's an abstract portrait of your . . . emotionally tortured cousin?'

'I don't think so, Al.'

'Well, how would he know what your cousin looks like?'

'What about Mum? She'd figure it out, she's so bloody suspicious. She keeps asking if she can see my drawings. Like she really gives a shit.'

'Tell your mum it's someone else from school, someone she doesn't know.'

'Good try, Al, but it's too complicated. What happened with Antonia has changed everything. You don't know what it's like, everyone watching you all the time, especially your mother, waiting for you to do something spooky.'

'So, what are you going to do?'

'I think I'll have to drop art.'

'What!'

'Maybe I could just drop my drawing elective. I could do photography, like you.'

'That's so sad. You love drawing and you're so talented.'

'You're right about me loving drawing,' Evie says, closing her eyes and finding pictures in her head. 'I think it has something to do with being an only child. When I was a kid I would sit there for ages, in my own little head space, drawing and chatting to myself. I didn't have anyone to play with, so I played with the people in my pictures,' she pauses. 'God, I was weird even then.'

'They should have flushed you down the loo at birth, girl-friend.'

Evie manages a little chuckle. She knows Alex is trying.

'Please don't tell anyone, Al. Not even Poppy. Okay?'

'Promise.'

'It's cold,' Evie pulls up the doona. 'My mother's about to get home.'

'Shit, it's nearly six o'clock,' Alex picks up her school bag. 'I've got to run. Are you going to be okay?'

'No,' Evie snorts. 'But I'll try and be. This is something

I'm going to have to work out on my own. But thanks, Al.'

Downstairs the front door unlocks.

'I told you.'

'Hello?' they hear her mother call.

'Piss off,' Evie sings back.

'Come down with me,' says Alex. 'Your mum'll be wondering what we've been doing.'

'Who gives a.'

'Come on,' Alex throws off the doona, takes Evie's ankles and starts to drag her off the bed. Evie holds on to the mattress.

'I'll drag you downstairs on the bed,' laughs Alex. She tugs hard. Evie and the mattress land on the floor. The girls squeal.

'What's going on?' says Robin, walking into the bedroom. 'Hi, Alex. What's the mattress doing on the floor?'

The girls can't control their giggling. They're becoming hysterical. Robin looks around the room. Her head stops as it spots Evie's pencils and sketchpad on the chair.

'So this is why you haven't managed to hand in your assignment. I thought you'd be taking it a bit more seriously.'

Powell has already phoned her.

Alex sneaks Evie a look. Evie rolls her eyes but her ears absorb the words.

'What's wrong with your eye?' Nick asks at breakfast time.

'Do you want coffee, Nick?'

'Thanks, Rob. Have you seen Evie's eye?'

'Do you want sugar or is this health-kick week?'

'No.' Nick shakes his head. 'Evie, come where the light's better. You probably have something in it.'

'An eyeball?' She steals Alex's pathetic joke.

'Robin? Can you have a look at Evie's eye? I can't see anything.'

'Look up. Down. To the side. The other side. No, I can't see anything,' she sighs, walking back to the coffee.

'Is it sore?'

'Not really,' replies Evie. 'But everything's a bit blurry.'

'Rob, do we have any eye drops?'

'Have a look in the bottom drawer of our bathroom.'

Robin drinks her coffee and reads the paper. She's still pissed off.

'Found some,' he calls. 'Now let's see,' he says, reading the directions. 'Two drops in affected eye every four hours.'

Gently, he pulls down the lower rim of Evie's left eye and squeezes in the drops.

'One, two. There we go.'

'Thanks, Dad.'

'Are you coming with me this morning?'

'No. I'll get the bus.'

'Evie?'

'Yes, Mum.'

'When's your next parent teacher meeting?'

'I don't know.'

'Well, I want to know when it is. Okay? So could you find out for me?'

'Yes.'

'How come?' asks Nick. 'Are we due for one?'

'Well, until Mr Powell phoned me yesterday it'd been a while since we've spoken to any of the teachers or seen the school counsellor.'

Evie senses that her mother is trying to calm her voice. It isn't working.

'I'd like to know how things are going, seeing Evie doesn't seem to tell us. Is anything wrong with that?'

'I wasn't saying that. You could . . .'

Evie doesn't hear their words. When the walls start closing in and their noise gets too loud, she presses the off button and doesn't feel a thing. It's all they seem to do these days – argue and blame. She knows she's their burden.

A lex is waiting for Evie at her locker. Her locker space is new. The old one has been stripped back, the hurtful words scrubbed away. It's now used as a second locker for a girl in Year 12 who plays the saxophone.

The only other time Alex waited at her locker this early was to announce she'd pashed Wazza Enright, one of the meathead footy players from Wolsley College.

'What's happened, Al?'

'I've got to show you something.' Alex's eyes flash and her voice sounds breathless. 'Hurry up!'

'What is it?'

'I had an early morning photography class. It was another developing session.'

'So?'

Alex's fingers are tapping her lips. 'Remember that night

at my house, after the markets and I took some photos of you in my bedroom?'

'Yes.' How can Alex imagine Evie could forget that day?

'Well, this morning I finished developing those photos.'

'And?' She doesn't know what Alex is going on about but there's a fear in the air she can almost touch. 'Just – tell – me, Alex.'

'Look, I've got to show you. It's completely freaky. Follow me.'

Steady and monotonous, the hum sings in Evie's head. The panic starts at her toes and creeps up her spine. She gulps the urge to start screaming and shouting.

Alex charges up the stairs, along a corridor and into the library. Evie runs behind holding the red cardigan tightly around her. She can hardly breathe. They go to a corner cubicle in the study room. Alex glances around, taking a small folder from under her jumper. Her eyes still flash and her hands shake as she tips the fresh black and white photos onto the desk.

'These are the ones of you.' Alex's hand slides the pile towards Evie. 'Have a look at them. Quickly.'

Evie picks up the photos. The sweat from her hands rubs onto the back of them, leaving a black smudge. She holds them up. Her left eye is still fuzzy but her right eye focuses clearly. She remembers the evening well. In the photo, she is sitting on Alex's bed looking surprised by the flash.

Then she sees it. Sees what Alex has seen. She pulls out the next photo and the next. It is there in every one, unmistakable. At first, it looks like a shadow, a bit of a blur. On second focus the shape is more defined. It looks like a human figure with long, matted hair. It stands behind Evie. It is the same in each photo.

'Can you see it?' Alex whispers.

Evie hands the photos back. Alex slips them into the folder and under her jumper.

'Who do you think it is?'

Evie shakes her head.

'It's definitely there. Isn't it?'

Evie says nothing.

'Do you think it's a woman?'

Evie shrugs.

'Do you know anyone with that sort of hair?'

She shakes her head again.

'Think!'

'I haven't a flipping clue who it is.' Evie tries to calm her voice. The panic is throbbing in her throat.

'Sorry, Evie.'

'Just say it.'

'What?'

'Come on!'

'What?'

'Just say it, Alex.'

'Say what?'

'Just say what you want to say!' shouts Evie.

'Shhh, Evie.'

Evie waits for her to speak. Alex stares at the ground.

'Ok, I'll say it,' she says eventually. 'Do you think it's the same girl as in your drawing?'

'I'm not sure.' Evie crosses her arms. 'Do you?'

Alex shrugs. 'No idea.'

'I know I've never seen the girl in the portrait or the photo. I promise, Alex.'

'I know. God, I wish there's someone who could help.'

'No way. Promise me you won't show those photos to anyone.'

'Promise. But, Evie, there has to be someone we can talk to?'

'There isn't. Trust me.'

The bell rings. The girls wander down to assembly in silence.

The hall is packed with the entire senior school. Girls are squealing, laughing and shoving each other. They stand there waiting to be seated while Evie concentrates on getting through the rest of the day.

'Do you reckon you'll say something to Powell about dropping your drawing elective?'

'No, not today. The portraits and the stupid proposal are due Thursday. Maybe I'll drop the bomb then.'

They pass the Year 12 CG from yesterday's canteen line. Evie feels the girl watch her.

At a safe distance she asks Alex, 'What did that girl say?'

'Nothing.'

'Tell me?'

'Don't you know?'

'No.'

Alex chooses seats at the end, away from the other Year 11 students. Evie faces her. She is not giving up. 'Come on. You have to tell me, Alex.'

'She said the canteen doesn't sell trips.'

Evie frowns.

'LSD, okay? Acid. Stupid, isn't it? I don't know why you wanted to know what the bitch said. They don't care.'

Evie thinks Alex is about to cry. She recognises the sign. The scar that runs from her nose to her lip is crinkled and trembles. Evie thinks about the times kids mimicked this twitching and chanted 'bunny, bunny'. Evie would tell them to get lost and take Alex's hand and lead her away from their teasing. She knows Alex has not forgotten this. They are bound together at the edge of the crowd.

'Are you all right, Al?'

Alex nods. 'Are you?'

Evie shrugs.

The headmistress arrives at the microphone and morning assembly commences.

'Can I still come to your place after school?'

'I thought you were anyway,' Alex replies. 'You can help me torture the brats.'

'I'll meet you at your locker.'

'Okay. Don't be late. I've got to get home quickly. Mum's got a session with her therapist at four.'

'Trevor Tryhard?'

'No, she dumped Trev. Mum says he burped too much.'

'Gross. I wonder if my mum thinks that?'

'Now she sees some woman called Andrea Ausbach.'

'Great name.'

'Andrea Ausbach,' Alex says again.

Alex's mum emerges from the bathroom wearing her famous red lipstick.

'You're home,' she says. 'Hi, Evie. How are you?'

'Good, thanks.'

'Now, I'm off to see Andrea.'

A smirk curls Evie's lip. If she looks at Alex she knows she'll start giggling.

'I'll be back by six. Your hair looks good like that, Evie. Alex, you should try wearing it up like that. I'm on my mobile if you want me.'

'Yes, Mum. I have done this before.'

'Don't forget to put the lasagne in the oven for the boys.'

'No, Mum.'

'Okay.' She blows them a kiss. 'Will you be here when I get home, Evie?'

'Probably not.'

'Well, bye, girls.'

'Bye.'

Fifteen minutes later Alex's brothers arrive home.

'I was not,' yells Tom, slamming the front door and stomping into the kitchen.

'You were so,' follows Dylan, chucking his bag on the floor. 'What's to eat?'

'Good afternoon, Dylan,' Alex says.

Dylan grunts. 'I'm hungry.'

'What's up your bum?' asks Evie. She loves the brats.

'A dick, that's what's up his bum,' calls Tom from the fridge.

Dylan runs at him and thumps him on the back. They end up rumbling on the kitchen floor. When Alex thinks Dylan is about to successfully strangle Tom with his school tie, she butts in.

'Get up off the floor, boys,' she yells. 'What's your problem, hey?'

'Dylan said I was acting gay on the bus,' pants Tom, smoothing down his hair.

'Well, you were,' spits Dylan. 'Dancing and singing like bloody Kylie.'

'What were you singing?' Alex asks.

Evie bursts into laughter. 'Yeah, which song was it?'

Alex starts singing. 'I bet it was "It's in your eyes".'

'Shut up,' shouts Tom. 'I was just singing.'

'And dancing,' adds Dylan. 'I can't wait for high school. I'll never have to catch the bus with you again.' He walks past Tom and pulls the stool from under him.

'You bloody dickhead,' shouts Tom. He chases his older brother through the house.

'Another lovely afternoon at the Lester household,' Alex says. 'Would you like to move in with us, Evie?'

'I like it here. You know that.'

'Oh, to be an only child like you!'

'Swap any day.'

'Come on, let the brats commit homicide in peace.'

Alex's bedroom is everything Evie's isn't. She has a four-poster bed with pink lacy curtains. Her teddies still sit on the windowsill and her walls are covered in posters of forgotten pre-teen idols.

'So are you going to try?' Alex asks.

'I don't know. What do you reckon?'

'Well, you could sketch me while we talk.'

'I suppose.'

'Maybe you could see if the face . . .?'

Evie can guess what Alex is suggesting. She has already considered the experiment but it's one she will do on her own.

'So should we try it?'

'I'm not sure, Al.'

'It mightn't happen this time.'

'But maybe it will.'

'Attitude, girlfriend.'

'I know, I know.' She hesitates for a second. 'Al? If I tell you something, do you promise not to think I've gone completely psycho?'

'Of course I won't.'

'I think . . .' Evie presses her fingers on her lips. She is afraid of hearing the words herself. She wants to tell Alex. Alex has become good at handling this stuff, she accepts it's part of their friendship. How lonely her life would be without Alex. 'I think,' she starts again. 'Shit, Al, this is going to sound so ridiculous.'

'Just tell me, Evie.'

'I think someone is trying to like, tell me something.'

'Who?'

'I'm not sure. 'I think I might mean like . . .'

'Like who?'

Evie presses her fingers against her lips. Harder this time

so she can feel the ridges of her teeth. 'Like, like – a dead person.'

Alex screams but recovers quickly. 'Sorry,' she squeaks.

'I told you you'd think I was weird.'

'I don't, I don't! I just, well, I just hadn't . . . hadn't thought of – that.'

'Look, it's this feeling I have. It's hard to describe. It's like somewhere in the back of my head there's a TV on that someone wants me to watch. But I don't want to watch it.' She pauses. 'You know, sometimes it feels like Antonia's brother was . . . was like my practice for this. If you get what I mean?'

'Evie, what are you going to do?' Alex gulps. 'I mean, this is, like, serious shit.'

'Let's see the photos again.'

'The photos?' Alex gasps. 'God, for a moment I forgot about those.'

As Evie lays the photos out on the desk she is struck by the fundamental difference between herself and Alex. It's so simple: Alex could forget, Evie never will.

The image of a human standing behind her seems almost clearer. She traces her finger around the transparent figure. She's certain this being wants to be seen. Like it master-minded the whole thing so it could show itself.

'Alex?' Evie must be careful with this request. 'Can I have these photos?'

'What? To keep?'

'Yes, to keep.' Again Evie concentrates on making her voice sound calm.

'Well, they are mine, you know.'

'I think it's better if I have them.'

Silence.

'Okay.'

Evie sees the wounded look on Alex's face, but she cannot risk it. She puts the photos in her school bag, checking the zipper twice.

'I wouldn't have shown them to anyone, Evie.'

'I trust you, Alex, you know that. I just think it's safer if I look after them.'

The girls sit in silence. It's already dark outside. The dread Evie felt yesterday starts to settle in her guts. And somewhere deeper than Evie has ever dared go she begins to understand that the dread will sit there until it's dealt with.

'Have you ever done one of those séances?' asks Alex.

'What, with a ouija board?'

'A what board?'

'A ouija board or some people call it a talking board, I think.'

'What on earth is that?'

'You've never heard of them?'

'Never,' says Alex. 'You know I've led a sheltered life.'

'Pull the other one.'

'So what do they do?'

'They help you communicate with the spirit world. They have letters and numbers around them and the spirits spell things out.'

'Is that how a séance works?'

'I think so,' Evie says. 'I've never done one before. I know my grandmother used to have a ouija board. I have a really vague memory of it. It was wooden with Egyptian drawings on it.'

'What happened to it?'

'My mum probably burnt it when Grandma died.'

'Your mum hated her, didn't she?'

A memory of Evie's grandma's house flashes through her mind. It's so vivid, almost like she's there. She can smell her grandma's rose perfume.

Evie is with her parents. Her grandma has been dead almost a week. They are going to sort through her belongings. Her father is quiet. Her mother is business-like. Evie wanders into her grandma's bedroom. It's the same as always: the blue bedspread is neat and smooth and the photo frames sit in the same position on her bedside table. Evie picks up her favourite one of her father as a little boy. His cheeks look round and soft. He is in his mother's arms and she is laughing and pressing her face against his.

Her parents go into the spare room. Her grandma called it Evie's room. She slept there when she stayed over. Her grandma made a Snow White bedspread especially for her. She can hear her mother: 'Well, that bangle's all she's having,' she is saying. Her father mumbles something she doesn't catch. The tension is seeping through the walls.

'Look, Nick, she's gone and as far as I'm concerned I never want to think of that hocus-pocus crap again.'

'Robin!' his voice is louder. 'You're sounding like your father.'

'I don't care. I want Evie to forget all of this,' her mother hissed. 'She is not going to turn out like her, Nick. Not if I can help it.'

A lex is saying something, but Evie is still in her grandma's bedroom. She looks up shaking her head. 'Sorry, Al? I wasn't listening.'

'You looked like you were seriously on another planet,' Alex replies. 'I said, are you sure you don't want to have a go at drawing me? See what happens?'

'No. I probably should get home.'

'Right now?'

'Hey, Al, when's Poppy back from Surfers?'

'I think her cousin's wedding is this weekend. I wish I had a grandma who lived on the Gold Coast.'

Evie nods.

'Poppy says she's going to line up us staying there for schoolies week next year. Pretty good, hey? Our own luxury accommodation while everyone else is cramped into the one motel room. I can live with that.'

Evie says nothing. She is afraid of tomorrow. Another year seems inconceivable.

B y the time Evie gets home she feels completely drained. All she can think about is going to bed. Switching off, time out.

'Dinner'll be ready in about half an hour,' her mum says.

'I'm not hungry,' replies Evie.

'Have it your own way.'

Evie stomps upstairs, chucks her bag in the doorway of her room and goes into the bathroom. She looks in the mirror. Her face is the younger version of her mother's. Their shells the same, their innards vastly different.

Her left eye looks worse. She covers her right eye and tries to focus but everything is fuzzy. She puts the bath on and undresses. Her skin is pale, not a winter pale; this has always been her complexion. She unties her hair. It spills onto her back and shoulders. She knows there are girls who envy her looks, who watch the movement of her svelte limbs and how she twirls her long ponytail around her fingers. If only they knew how quickly she would trade them in.

She flinches as she pulls her hair into a bun. There's a lump on the back of her head. She runs her hand over it, catching her fingers in a knot.

'Ouch,' she says, trying to untangle the hairs.

The bath is warm. The water swirls around her neck. She closes her eyes, trying to ignore the dread that nags.

It's not even light when she wakes. Evie gets up and starts the homework that is piling up on her desk. She opens up *Macbeth*, but William Shakespeare has trouble capturing her attention.

She looks at the poem they're studying, *The Rime of the Ancient Mariner*, by Samuel Taylor Coleridge. It's eerie but

she likes it. The words in Part VI move her. It's when the
mariner wakes up from a trance and the curse is finally
broken. Evie wonders what it'd be like if her curse were
lifted. Would she know? Would she feel it? 'Like one, that
on a lonesome road,' she starts to recite. 'Doth walk in fear
and dread.'

For a while she doesn't notice she is drawing on the page.
It's not until a shape emerges over the words that she
realises. Her hand works quickly, sketching and shading.
It's as if the pencil is controlling her arm. It directs which
way the lines and curves join. The only noise is the scratch-
ing of lead on paper. The pencil draws faster and darker,
its path running over the words onto the next page. Her
hand is beginning to hurt. She can feel sweat between her
fingers. She tries to stop. The pencil is piercing a hole in
the page.

Evie lurches forward as though she is falling. The pencil
flies out of her hand and she sits back panting. Her hand
covers the page. She counts the thumps in her chest, 'One,
two, three.' Slowly she slides her hand away, hoping to
smudge what is under there – 'Four, five.' She sneaks a look.
'Six.'

It's not what she expects. The face she fears isn't there.
Covering her left eye she tries to make out the shapes the
pencil drew. Three cylinders sitting above four triangles.
That's all.

Evie puts the book in a drawer and flops back into bed
pulling the doona over her head. A strange smell sits on her
hands. She sniffs them again. It's not the familiar lead-like

smell. It's like grass clippings from a lawnmower. Evie tucks her hands under the pillow and tries to sleep.

'Your eye looks terrible,' her mother says to her at break-fast. 'Have you been using those eye drops?'

'Sort of,' shrugs Evie. 'Has Dad gone already?'

'He and Theo had some work breakfast.'

Evie stares into the fridge.

'Don't just leave the fridge door open. What are you looking for?'

'I'm not sure. I'm not really hungry.'

'Evie, you didn't have any dinner last night. What's going on?'

'Nothing, Mum. I'm just not hungry.'

'Did you find out the date of the next parent teacher meeting?'

'Oops, I forgot. Sorry.' She watches her mother behead a carrot, hack it into little pieces, and throw it into a saucepan on the stove.

'I'm going to take you to school this morning,' she announces.

Evie looks up from the bowl of cereal she is playing with.

'We'll stop by the chemist to get something for your eye and then I'll personally go and find out when the next parent teacher meeting is.' She glances at her watch. 'I want to leave in fifteen minutes.'

Evie stares into her cereal seeing the clay figures in the art room.

At the chemist her mother pulls her eyelid in every possible direction. The pharmacist leans against her, umming and aahing, trying to get a good look.

'Hmm. It's very inflamed,' she states.

Derr, thinks Evie.

'It might be worth going to the GP,' the pharmacist continues. 'I can't actually see anything in it.'

'No, neither can I.' Robin has almost turned Evie's eye inside out. 'We're in a rush to get to school. Could you show me what other drops we could try?'

They walk away, leaving Evie at the counter. Her eye bounces back into its socket.

'Agh!' She blinks, trying to get it back to its rightful position. 'Maybe you'd like to take my eyeball with you.'

Robin spins around. 'Beg your pardon, Evie?'

She's quick, thinks Evie. She never misses a thing.

As they walk through the school playground, Evie feels eyes on them. She knows her mother does, too. She virtually has to jog to keep up with her long, fast strides.

'Where's your first class?'

Evie points up the stairs to the library.

'Well, I'm going to the school office. I'll see you tonight.' Her mother is talking quickly. 'By the way, I'll be late home. I forgot to tell your father. There's a casserole in the crockpot.'

Evie's stomach pops with panic.

'Bye, Mum.'

Evie and Alex sit together in the library's video room, watching a documentary on China.

'God, your eye looks bad,' whispers Alex.

'I had the full-on humiliating experience at the chemist this morning.'

'Don't you love them.'

'My mother just about took my eyeball out.'

'Was it the chemist in Darley Parade?'

'Yep.'

'I love the old girl there with the white, squeaky shoes. She always asks, "Dear, do you want your feminine hygiene products in a bag?" "No, lady," I'm going to say one of these days. "I'm going to hang the tampons on my ears." '

They start laughing.

'Sshhh,' a girl says behind them.

They pull a face and pretend to watch the video.

Last period of the day is art theory. Tomorrow, Evie's major work proposition and portraits are due. Her sore eye could not have come at a better time. She is going to bat her red eye in Powell's face and explain how impossible it has been to do any drawing. In fact, she'll use it as the excuse for all her overdue work.

Evie gets to class early. Powell is already there, going through a sheet of slides. The way he leans over the desk allows Evie a good perve at the bald patch on top of his head. She coughs. He looks up, and she can tell by the jerk of his body that she has given him a fright. She presses her lips together to hide the smile.

'Yes, Evie?' he says.

She stares into his face. Her left-sided vision is hazy, making him look like he has only half a nose.

'Yes, Evie?' he repeats.

'Sir, my eye has been very sore this week,' she speaks in a soft voice. 'I can't really see out of it.'

She watches him nod and fold his arms. Now she can see the smirk that sits inside his lips.

'Um, I haven't been able to do much work on my portraits.'

'Well, you'll just have to bring in what you have done. I haven't seen anything yet,' he replies. 'I've spoken to your mother, as you know, and of course she's very – concerned.'

'I know, sir. Just a couple of days, please? It is my first attempt after, well after . . .' She swallows and jumps in. 'After, you know, and I'm, I'm . . .'

His eyes have not left hers. He rolls back on his heels and puts his hands in the pockets of his black jeans. 'I'll think about it,' he says.

On the way home, Evie stares out the window of the school bus. She wonders how many times in the past twelve weeks she has done exactly this, never noticing anything, just staring, trying to digest the disasters of the day. When she first returned to school she hoped things would improve. She knows better now.

'Hi, Evie.'

Seb is wrestling himself and his double bass into the seat next to her.

'Is Poppy still away?'

'Yep,' Evie says, turning around to face him.

'Shit!' Seb shouts. 'Your eye!'

Evie's cheeks flush.

'Sorry,' he says. 'It's just really red.'

'Don't worry about it.'

It's only then that Evie realises Seb has got on the bus a few stops early.

'Hey, where have you come from?' she asks.

'We had orchestra practice with Saint Martha's.'

'Oh.'

Some boys down the back of the bus start yelling at each other. Kids turn around and stand up to watch the fight erupting. Evie and Seb stay in their seats and Evie wonders why Seb doesn't want to watch the testosterone show. He seems more intent on watching her.

'Do you know them?' She gestures behind her.

'Huh?'

'Do you know them?' she shouts.

The noise on the bus is bouncing off the windows. Any minute and the driver will stop the bus and start shouting, too. When they get to the pin, Seb's usual stop, the driver slams on the brakes.

'I'll throw you all off the bus if you don't shut up,' he yells.

There is a second of silence followed by some heckling. The boys from Wolsley College file down the aisle, wondering what drama they missed. Rather than looking out the window, Evie watches them. The bus pulls away with a jerk and the shouting starts up again. Someone chucks a hat, then a shoe. There's a chant starting up and a girl is squealing.

Seb leans over and whispers something to Evie.

'What?' she yells. 'I can't hear you.'

He shakes his head and turns around to watch the fight.

Walking up the driveway Evie hears the phone ringing inside. She wrestles with the lock and runs to the kitchen. The answering machine has turned on but the person has hung up. She goes to the stove and lifts the lid off the crockpot. God, she hates her mother's casseroles. They smell of dog food.

The phone starts ringing again.

'Hello,' Evie says.

There is silence at the other end.

'Hello?'

She can hear someone breathing.

'Evangaline?'

'Who is this?'

There's no reply, just breathing.

'Hello? Who is this?'

'Evangaline?' the voice starts up again. 'You don't know me. My name is Victoria. I was a friend of your grandmother, Anna.'

Silence.

'Are you still there?'

'Yes,' Evie whispers as her knees give way into the chair.

'This will sound strange,' Victoria begins. 'I had to ring you. I feel as though you're in some trouble. Are you okay?'

'How . . . how did –?' Evie stops, realising the answer.

'Your grandma and I were kindred spirits.'

'God,' is all Evie manages. She has never heard of this lady,
Victoria.

'Can you come and see me on the weekend?'

'Um?'

'I live in Randwick. There's a bus from Wynyard that goes
almost to my door.'

'I probably could. Why?'

'It's important. I feel you need some guidance. Do you
understand what I mean by that?'

'I . . . I think so.'

'Yes, you do. Anna had a little word to me.'

The simplicity of the statement makes Evie dizzy.

'Does my grandma – talk to you?'

'Quite a lot, actually.'

'She's never –'

'Evangaline, you're young. Your gift is young.'

Evie closes her eyes. These words mean everything.

'It doesn't feel like a gift.'

'Not yet, dear.'

'It doesn't even feel real.'

'That's because you lack confirmation.'

'Confirmation?'

'Yes, validation.' Her voice is soft and reassuring. 'To put
it simply, dear, you feel like people think you're a fraud,
a pretender.'

'Exactly!'

'But I'll tell you something for nothing – that's a psychic's
joke,' laughs Victoria. 'Your gift was validated by someone
just today.'

'What?'

'Give it some thought.'

'But no one has said anything to me ever about – it.'

'Who is the tall boy?'

'I'm not sure what you –?'

'He carries something, like a large black case.'

'Seb?'

'Maybe.'

'I sat next to him on the school bus, just a few minutes ago. He didn't say anything. He wouldn't know a thing about – you know, me.'

'Think hard, then. Maybe it was someone else.'

'Okay.'

'So you'll come?'

'I'll try.'

'You will.' Victoria gives Evie her address and the bus numbers.

'I'll see you Saturday, if not before,' she says. 'And do give that tall boy some thought. I feel it is him.'

Evie's hands shake as she hangs up the phone. Thoughts are colliding and exploding in her head like thunderbolts.

'*Oh my god!*' she suddenly yells.

As though hearing the words for the first time, she has just realised what Seb whispered to her on the bus. She looks at her watch. It was less than fifteen minutes ago. She closes her eyes and tries to calm her mind. She is desperate for the memory. They are nearing the pin, Seb's usual stop. But today he is already on the bus. She watches the other boys file down the aisle. She doesn't want to look out the window.

She hates looking out there. The bus pulls away. It's so noisy – the fight has started up the back again. Seb is watching her. He leans over and whispers something in her ear. She can hear him clearly now, as though he is sitting next to her.

She says his words out loud. 'Do you still see her?'

Evie steams some rice and sets the table for dinner. The smile stretches her cheeks. It's like having a secret no one else knows. Tonight she has her father all to herself and there are things she must ask him. She needs to know enough to fill in the gaps, but not enough to start him wondering. She folds the serviettes, forming the questions in her head.

'Did Robin say she was going to therapy?'

'She wouldn't tell me that, Dad. She just said she'd be late home.'

'Actually, she's probably setting exams,' he says. 'The semester ends next week. She's been so busy.'

Evie nods and thinks how time has crawled.

'The table looks nice. What's the catch, hey?'

'Mum's famous crockpot casserole.'

'Oh.'

'Never fear, I've made some rice and a humungous salad.'

'It's times like this we need a dog.'

'Dad!'

Evie serves up dinner.

'My, service, too.'

'What brekkie did you and Theo have this morning?'

She sits down and passes her dad the pepper.

'A very boring breakfast with a very boring speaker. Thank god Theo asked a thousand questions or it would've been a complete flop.'

'You can always rely on Theo for that.'

'The Bircher muesli was good, though.'

'How long have you and Theo been friends, Dad?'

'Oh, let's see,' he counts on his fingers. 'Close to forty years, I reckon.'

'Wow. I wonder if Al and I will still be friends after that long?'

'I suppose it depends on how much the friendship means to you. Theo's always been like the brother I never had and he's good friends with your mum, too. That makes a difference.'

'Was Grandma friends with Theo's mother?'

'Eleni? Yes, they were friends, not really close but they were friends. I remember Dad'd play bowls with Theo senior sometimes. But Eleni was the superstitious one; the Greeks tend to be a bit that way. She enjoyed Mum's company, especially her insights.'

Evie finds the gap she is waiting for. 'Did Grandma have any friends who were like, you know, the same as her?'

'Yes.' She watches her father put down his fork and pick up his wine, swirling the red liquid around the glass. 'Yes. She did have a good friend, although they didn't meet until much later. In fact, I think you were already born. They became very close, probably because they had so much in common. They were mothers, wives and yet they shared this extraordinary gift.'

96

'What was she like?'

'You know, I only met her a few times. My mum talked about her a lot, so I felt like I knew her well. I sometimes wonder what happened to her.'

Evie gets up and takes the plates to the sink.

'What was her name?' She holds her breath.

'Victoria. Victoria Gaunt.'

Evie closes her eyes, feeling the tap-water warm her hands.

'Thank you,' she whispers.

The next morning Evie is up early. She only has this one chance. She washes her hair, rehearsing what to say to Seb. The knot at the back of her head feels bigger. Looking in the mirror she holds it up.

'I've got a dreadlock.' She rakes the comb through the matted lock but it gets caught. 'Ouch!'

With the comb hanging from her hair, she steps into the shower to get the conditioner. She rubs a bit into the knot. It feels wet and sticky.

'Yuck.'

Evie wipes the steam off the mirror. Beyond it something moves, expanding and shrinking into itself. It looks like a person trying to step out of their skin. In a flash it's gone, leaving only the reflection of herself.

'You're off early,' Nick says.

'I've got some things to do in the library,' Evie lies.

'That cardigan's filthy, Evie. Give it to me and I'll wash it.'

'It's fine, Mum.'

'You haven't had breakfast and your lunch isn't ready.'

'Don't worry. I'll get something at the canteen.' She grabs her bag and escapes.

She has fifteen minutes to get to Seb's bus stop. She walks fast along the footpath, counting each step till she reaches a corner. She knows what she's going to say. She just wishes she knew what he'll say. It is a risk, she understands this, but everything she feels about Seb predicts it will be okay.

The terrace houses merge into their neighbours' as Evie's pace quickens. She looks at her watch, seven minutes left. Her legs work faster, the steam shoots from her mouth. She turns the last corner and spots him just ahead.

'Seb,' she calls. 'Wait.'

She feels self-conscious running up to him. She has never been this eager to see him before. His look is puzzled but he waits.

'Are you okay?' he asks.

She is panting and there are drops of sweat on her forehead. 'Yeah, yeah.'

'Sure?'

She suddenly feels awkward, standing here in front of him.

'Seb,' she begins, trying to calm her voice. 'I really need to ask you something.'

'What?'

He is walking towards the bus stop.

'Um, Seb. Can we just wait here a minute? I don't want to, well, this is, you know, kind of private.'

'What?'

'God, this is really, um . . . Look, I'm just going to say it. Yesterday, on the bus, you whispered something to me.'

The recognition washes over his face.

'You remember that, don't you?'

He nods. She sees his Adam's apple jump.

'You asked me if I still see her, didn't you?'

He nods again.

'Please, Seb, please tell me what you meant. It's . . .' She hesitates. 'It's very, very important to me.'

'My mum once told me . . .' Now he hesitates. 'That you . . . you sometimes used to – to see a girl at – the pin.'

Evie grabs hold of the fence.

'Your mum? But how? How did your –?'

'I don't know. Someone must have told her.'

He slides down the fence and sits on his bag. Evie does the same.

'I don't know a hell of a lot about it, Evie. I mean, I know a girl died there.'

'What?'

'A girl died there, at the pin. I thought it was the one you – you . . .'

'A girl *died* there!' The lump rises through her chest into her throat. She mouths the air. 'Are, are . . .'

'What? You didn't know?'

'No, I didn't.' Evie's jaw is trembling. 'When? When was it?'

'I think we were probably three or four. It was a hit and run. Evie, I don't –'

She shakes her head to stop his words. The lump is so tight now she feels like throwing up. Seb sits there, staring at his hands. Evie's sure he understands what's just happened. It's like there is nothing they can say. It's too big.

They hear the bus coming around the corner. Seb stands up, throwing his bag over his shoulder.

'Come on, Evie.' He holds out his hand to her.

She looks up at him and shakes her head.

'Evie?'

'I'm okay, Seb. I think I'll just hang here for a while.'

He runs to catch up with the bus. She watches him watching her, until the bus is out of sight.

Evie sits on the ground, holding her head. Her brain sounds like fireworks. Hot tears sting her eyes. She wants to cry, she wants to howl and scream and yet somewhere she wants to jump for joy. She opens her diary planner. Her hands shake as she flicks through the pages to the note she made yesterday: 24/211 Lancet St, Randwick. Take the 503 bus from Wynyard and get off at car wash in Randwick. Corner of second street on left.

At the bus stop she wedges her bag between her feet to steady her. The traffic whizzes by but everything looks and feels like slow motion. Even the noise on the road has slowed to a weird, echoing drone. The step on the bus seems higher, the driver's nose looks too long, and the machine takes forever to spit out her ticket.

Evie stumbles onto the bus, taking a seat on the right-hand side. As the pin approaches she turns and stares out the window. The girl isn't there.

This time, Evie's eyes follow a barricade that runs the length of the sharp bend. She realises she has never considered why the barricade is there. But now she knows. She calculates that at least twelve years ago a young girl was killed here. But she still has to see it for herself.

At Hyde Park Evie gets off and runs to the state library. She's done this for school assignments at least a hundred times. It'll take ten minutes, fifteen tops. She chucks her bag in a locker and finds the newspaper drawer marked 1991. The roll for March is the first one she spots. She grabs it, hooking it onto the machine. Madly scrolling through sport sections and classifieds, the days of March 1991 rush before her.

Nothing. She takes out May, July, December, September and does the same.

Click – it's there, 25 September 1991: 'Girl Killed in Hit and Run'. The top paragraph of 'News in Brief'. The words are jumping off the page like tiny black fleas. 'Notorious bend – the pin – Bridgepoint Road – seven years old – massive blood loss – head injuries – killed instantly.'

Evie's fingers won't cooperate as she tries to roll up the reel. She attempts to stuff it into the box but it keeps spilling out. She shoves it into the drawer and bolts.

Back at Hyde Park, she waits for the 503 to Randwick. It's due in eight minutes. First period is nearly finished. She checks her timetable – a geography documentary. She won't be missed. Alex has a late start on Thursday mornings.

Evie digs around the bottom of her bag for the eye drops. Her hands still shake as she squirts the drops in her left eye, most of it running into her mouth, their coolness still soothing the ache. She blinks, washing them through the redness and as she does a blurred pattern of shapes appears on the footpath. Three cylinders above four triangles, just like the ones in her drawing. When she blinks again they disappear.

The 503 approaches. The square cabin of the bus speeds towards her and a thundering clamour shakes beneath her feet. Evie feels like she is falling, falling between the wheels. She screams and jumps back.

'Are you all right?'

'What?' Evie looks up. A lady is touching her arm. The others in the queue look embarrassed. She takes her arm away. 'Yeah. I'm okay.'

Evie hides in the corner of the back seat. A grassy smell lingers. She sniffs the end of her plait, thinking it must be the chemist brand shampoo. What Victoria will look like and all the things they will talk about drift through her mind. Evie feels peaceful, almost sleepy. Closing her eyes she hears the rumbling of the wheels and the squeal of the brakes as the bus takes her up Elizabeth Street to Randwick.

She is not what Evie expects. Victoria is tall. Her eyes are large and brown and blink slowly as she speaks.

'I thought I might see you today,' she says softly. 'Come in. Dear, dear, your eye is very red. I wonder what that means?'

Evie steps into a small room wall-to-wall with photos. A cookbook is open on the table and the crossword in the newspaper is half done.

'Would you like a cup of tea, Evangaline?'

'Thanks. That'd be great.' She contemplates saying 'everyone calls me Evie', but decides not to. She likes Evangaline, at least today she does.

Evie follows Victoria into the kitchen. Jars of preserved lemons line the shelves.

'Are you hungry? I've got some fruit bun.'

'I didn't have breakfast,' Evie remembers. 'It's been, let's say, a very weird morning.'

'Well, let's sit down and have a cuppa and some bun. Then, we can have a long chat. Should you be at school?'

Evie goes to speak.

'Not important. I feel much better now you're here, Evangaline. We've been worried.'

They go back to the little sitting room. Victoria pushes the heater closer to the table. Evie feels the warm air blowing on her legs. She eats her bun, then washes it down with perhaps the most fantastic cup of tea she's ever tasted. She laps up the comfort of this moment. She could just lie down on the floor and sleep.

'There's plenty more bun.'

'No thanks,' Evie replies, yawning and stretching her legs. 'That was perfect.'

'Do you feel tired?' Victoria asks. 'When things are

happening,' she makes a wide circle around her head. 'It can be very exhausting.'

Evie nods in agreement and the realisation dawns that in this room, at this very moment, she is free. The feeling is as powerful as it is peaceful.

'You were right about yesterday,' Evie says. 'About someone – what was the phrase you used?'

'Validating your gift, is what I think I said.'

'Yeah, that's it,' says Evie. 'And it was Seb. He's the tall boy on the bus.'

'And how did you feel?'

'Weird. Confused. Kind of happy.'

'So what happened? What did he say?'

'It's unbelievable. I don't know what to think.' Evie tells her about the little girl at the pin. Victoria leans across the table, nodding her head, as Evie describes the first time she saw her.

'That's my first memory of anything, you know, strange,' explains Evie. 'It took me till I was nearly eight to realise no one else saw her. I know how ridiculous it must sound but I really didn't understand.' She stops and thinks. 'I don't understand why Grandma or someone didn't tell me.'

'She couldn't,' Victoria answers.

'But why couldn't she? It would have made things so much easier.' The hot tears sting again. 'I didn't know what I was seeing or hearing half the time. I still don't, I just live with it.' Evie blows her nose. 'It sucks that it takes Seb to tell me the truth. That a girl really died there. Even he knew I saw her, god knows how.'

'Evangaline, it was very complicated. I first met Anna, your grandma, just around that time. Your grandpa had just died. She was in despair over losing him and she was in despair about what to do with you.'

Evie is sobbing now. She cannot stop the tears. Years of them fly everywhere, spilling down onto her red cardigan.

'I'll tell you a little about what I know.' Victoria's hands hold Evie's. 'But some of the other things –' Evie senses a hesitation in her voice. 'You'll have to speak to your father about.'

Evie understands the deal. It's the only deal she's had so far.

Victoria begins to tell her a story. The sound of her voice is soothing as it gently guides Evie back to her childhood.

'Anna rang me the first time you saw the girl at the pin. She was upset and confused about what to do. Your dad had told her how your mother became difficult – impossible – about it. She forbade Anna or your father to say anything to you about it.

'You see, the year before a seven-year-old girl had been killed there by a hit and run. She died of massive head injuries. It was in all the local papers. It was horrible.

'According to Anna, it was the first time you ever displayed your special sense, your gift. Before then no one knew whether you had it or not. You see, Nick didn't get it and seeing he was Anna's only child, she had to wait till the next generation to see if it'd been passed down. But your mother would not allow you to be told. Anna and Nick thought initially it was some type of denial, that she would change her mind. She never did. It caused your grandmother and your father enormous worry keeping it from you. But what could they do?

'And I think Nick felt so terrible, so guilty about you getting it from his side of the family that he just blindly obeyed everything your mother said. In the end he made Anna swear that she would respect your mother's wishes. Because, after all, she was your mother and she had the final say. What's her name again?'

Evie can barely form her lips around the word. 'Robin.'

'Yes, that's right.' Victoria's brown eyes narrow and focus on her. Evie shifts in her seat. She feels she is about to hear why she's been told all of this.

'Evangaline, I have told you what is really none of my business. But I have told you because I think it's time you understood your gift. You see, there is something truly special about you. Tell me, what is going on? As I said on the phone, Anna and I sense trouble around you. And, I'm not sure, but I don't think I'm necessarily talking about emotional trouble. Do you understand what I'm saying, Evangaline? There is a powerful energy around you. It wants you.'

Evie swallows hard. She's not certain where to start. She knows it's her turn to speak but what to say? Her thoughts are tumbling.

'I think I know what you mean. There's stuff going on that I don't have a clue about.'

Evie feels a heat. It rises up through her chest and into her throat. She pushes it back. She has to get rid of this burden.

Victoria squeezes her hand. 'You're safe here.'

'It started in April, when I drew a girl's portrait. But, I didn't actually end up drawing her.' Evie bites her lip. It's still so hard to say. 'I ended up drawing her . . . her – dead brother. I don't know how it happened. I didn't even know she had a brother or anything. Now I feel like it's happening again but much worse. I keep drawing a young woman's face and I don't know who it is.'

Evie tastes the blood as she bites her lip harder. 'I'm,' she swallows, 'terrified.'

Victoria stands up and takes the mugs and plate to the kitchen. Evie hears her filling the sink with water and the squirt of a detergent bottle. Why has Victoria walked away? She isn't sure if she is meant to follow. She doesn't understand the rules. She's a novice.

'Evangaline?' calls Victoria. 'I want you to make a list of what's been happening.'

'A list?'

'Try and put it in sequence, you know, what happened first then next, then next and so on.'

Victoria walks into the sitting room, wiping the soapsuds from her fingers.

'Do you need some paper?' she asks. 'I think what you should do is get a little diary and start recording things as you observe them. And dreams, when an energy is strong like that, the dreams can be important, too.'

'Do you think there's –?'

'Evangaline,' says Victoria. 'The energy is so strong I had to walk out of the room. What you're feeling is real.'

Evie pulls her homework diary out of her bag, then squashes it back in. 'As if,' she scoffs.

'You must be careful,' Victoria says, searching through a cupboard. 'There are very few people you can trust.

Unfortunately, your mother is not one of them. Not this time. The tall boy has had his use. Your father is safe and there's another man. He has a strong perfume. You also have a good friend.'

'Alex?'

'But remember it's a lot to tell another girl who doesn't really understand it, the way you and I do. She was dealt an unfair hand at birth. She craves normality.'

Victoria's voice is muffled as she continues searching through the cupboard.

'The true sceptics are easy to pick,' she says. 'They watch your every move, waiting to catch you out. Remove yourself from them, for they will suck your energy dry.'

Victoria takes an exercise book and a box wrapped in newspaper out of the cupboard. She puts the box on the table and passes Evie the exercise book.

'Here, this can be your diary. I'm going to finish the washing up. I want you to write the list and then we'll go through it.'

Evie flattens the first page and writes, Wednesday, April 10th. Antonia Cipri.

The day she will lug around forever.

She checks her diary for the other dates.

Friday, June 12th. Start working on Alex's portraits.

Saturday, June 13th. Alex takes photos of me in her room (figure in the photos).

She flips through her diary, trying to find the exact date the first portrait changed.

Thursday, June 18th. (I think) first portrait changed.

'How are you going?' Victoria calls.

'I can't think of anything else,' Evie says, looking at her pathetic list. 'Hang on, I drew these shapes the other night when I was reading a poem. It was like the pencil had control over my hand. I saw them again today, on my way here.'

'What sort of shapes?'

'Cylinders and triangles. Weird.'

'Note them down.'

Tuesday 27th June. My pencil drew three cylinders above four triangles.

Thursday 29th June. Saw the shapes at the bus stop.

Victoria studies the list for a few minutes. Evie sits there, thinking how weird this all is and yet how normal it seems, too.

'What about your eye, Evangaline? You haven't mentioned it.'

'My eye?' Evie's hand cups her eye. 'I hadn't really thought of that.'

'I mean, is this a condition you get or is it new?'

'No, no,' Evie answers. 'I've never had it before. It just kind of started and it's definitely got worse.'

'When did it start? Look at your list,' she taps the open page. 'See if it prompts any memories.'

'Victoria?' Evie stares at the dates. 'I think it started with the portraits of Alex.'

'Jot it down, Evangaline.'

'God.' Evie wipes her hands on her cardigan and writes next to the June 12th entry – 'eye starts to go blurry'.

'Do you remember any dreams during this time?'

'Actually I had a really weird dream about a girl trying to

pull my cardigan off. She had long, dark reddish hair.' Evie rubs the back of her head. 'Her hair was all matted and –' Her fingers touch the sticky knot in her own hair. 'Oh, my god,' she gasps.

'What?' asks Victoria. 'Have you remembered something?'

'My hair,' she whispers. 'I've had a knot. This sticky, matted – it's almost like a dreadlock. It keeps getting bigger. That started about the same time as my eye, too.'

Victoria runs her hand over it. 'Look, it could be a connection. Messages come in many different forms. Write it down and the dream.'

She feels Victoria watching her as she writes. She's not sure if Victoria's calm voice and businesslike manner are for real or whether she's trying to hide the fact that she's totally freaking out, too.

'In the dream, was it the cardigan you're wearing now?'

'Well, it was in the beginning but then the buttons turned into these little blue teddies, like a cardigan I had as a kid. The girl said "that's mine", something like that.'

'Is there anything special about this cardigan?' Victoria leans over and feels the cuff. 'What's it made of?'

'Cashmere. I've got a bit of a thing about vintage clothes. Dad got it in Adelaide.'

'Have you had any other sensations with clothes?'

Evie tells Victoria about the shawl incident at the markets. 'The actual shawl didn't feel strange, I did. And these words just sort of blurted from my mouth like it was someone else talking. I couldn't stop them. I was too freaked out to ask but I have a feeling I even spoke with an accent.'

'Ah, that's called psychometry. It's sensing something through an object that once belonged to someone else. It's like you feel their emotions. It's a very powerful form of communication.'

Evie feels a shiver run from the top of her head to the soles of her feet. 'Do you think –?' She stops mid sentence. The idea is too great.

'That the cardigan might have something to do with it?' Victoria finishes her thought.

Evie's mouth opens. No sound comes out.

'Evangaline.' Victoria takes her hand. 'I'm not sure. There are always coincidences. However, your sketching is a powerful vehicle. That I'm sure of, and that is what you have to focus on. Write down or draw any pictures or words that come to you. Sometimes they're just flashes and you need to catch them before they're out of focus. Does that make sense? You have to approach this methodically, almost like a detective.' Victoria holds up the diary. 'It's these signs that will lead you there. Don't be afraid of them, it's their only way of communicating. They're not meant to frighten you. They're meant to lead you. Remember this, Evangaline, if it is the only thing you do: follow the signs no matter how, how strange they may seem.'

'God, I feel like I'm doing a crash course in psychic phenomena.' Evie surprises herself by laughing.

'Well, you are,' agrees Victoria.

'You know, sometimes I feel so scared and then there are times when I understand that maybe I'm just the same as Grandma and that helps for a while.'

'You are, my dear, and she was very special, just like you.'

'But it doesn't feel special. It feels awful. My head has seriously been flipping out and the worst thing is it's so exhausting trying to act – you know – normal.'

'Well, rest assured, dear, it's not you,' she says. 'Someone is trying to get you to take notice. Of what, I'm not sure. But it will let you know when it's time. Just let your senses guide you. It may be a smell, a sound, a feeling; trust in your own intuition for it's you that's been given the gift.'

Victoria unwraps the newspaper and hands her a wooden box. Evie recognises it immediately.

'Grandma's ouija board!'

'I've had it all this time and now I want to give it to you.'

Evie traces her fingers around the tiny Egyptian figures.

'Wow,' she gasps. 'This is so special. Thank you. You know, I have a memory of this board.'

'It's a beautiful board. It's from the 1940s.'

'Vintage!'

'Yes,' chuckles Victoria. 'One hundred per cent vintage.'

'Now I've got two things of Grandma's.'

'What's the other thing?'

'Her silver bangle.'

'Oh my god! The square one from St Petersburg?'

'Yes. Do you know it?'

'Anna never took it off. You must wear it. My god, if I know you're wearing that I'll sleep much better.'

'Do you think I should do a séance?'

'If you do, it is only to be with me. Okay?'

'Okay.'

'There are rules even with séances.'

'Like what?'

'Well, let's see. A clear night is preferable. Definitely not when there are any eclipses. When an entity speaks you must be silent and you have to get their permission to ask questions. The list goes on and on.'

'How will I know if I need to do one?'

'You will, Evangaline. Now, I want you to keep this somewhere safe. Not wanting to sound like a bad influence but do not let your mother know this ouija board is in the house. The consequences will seem massive and for a while they will be.'

'I can imagine,' Evie scoffs.

'If you believe in yourself, even in your darkest moments, she will come to believe in you, too.' Victoria nods. 'Yes, she will.'

'No way, you don't understand. She hates anything to do with this, including me.'

'She loves you, Evangaline, but she's found all this very hard to accept and yet there are reasons she should be thankful to Anna.'

'She wishes I was different. I know that. The one thing about being like this is that people are so, so transparent. Sometimes it's like I can see straight through them.'

'I know dear. It's hard to make friends, being like this.'

Evie almost floats out of Victoria's flat. Outside the sun warms her back and a voice whispers in her ear, 'This is who you are. This is who you are.'

She nurses the ouija board, which is now in a black plastic bag. A part of her, the old part, plans a safe hiding spot. The other part absorbs an energy that is surrounding her body, peeling back her skin, allowing a new being to emerge and step forth, and that part isn't scared.

When she gets off the bus, she checks her wallet. It's crazy but it's what she wants to do. She strolls up to the counter of the corner store and asks for a packet of ciggies and a box of matches. She peels off the plastic and reads the warning sign: SMOKING IS A HEALTH HAZARD.

'So is having a mother like mine,' she says to the packet.

She takes one out, lights it and inhales the deceit. 'I'll never forgive you,' she whispers. 'I'll never forgive you for keeping from me who I really am.'

Evie puts the ouija board on the floor and drags the chair over to her bedroom cupboard. She leans into the top shelf. If she can shift the suitcases over a bit she'll be able to slip the ouija board behind them. She tries to push the first suitcase over but there isn't enough room for both hands. The phone starts to ring. The answering machine clicks over.

'Hi, you've called the Simmons household.' She hears her mother echo through the house. 'We can't get to the phone right now . . .'

Evie mimics her voice, 'As I'm a little busy tampering with the truth. Please leave a message at your own risk.'

Alex interrupts her fun. 'Are you there, Evie? It's me? Pick up the phone.'

Evie runs into her parents' room and grabs the receiver.
'Alex!'

'Why are you puffing?'

'I just ran to the phone 'cause I heard your voice.'

'Where were you?'

'I was up the top of my cupboard.'

'What? No, I mean today, where were you?'

'Alex, you will not believe what's happened. Today has been one of the most amazing days in my whole entire life. I promise, I am not exaggerating.'

'What happened?'

'Well, like at the moment I'm mucking around the top shelf of my cupboard so I can hide – get ready for it – my grand-mother's ouija board.'

'What!'

'It's a long, long story. I wagged today –'

'You wagged?'

'Yep and it's the best thing I've ever done.'

'You've gone mad!'

'No, I've gone unmad. I also bought a packet of ciggies.'

'You don't even smoke, you dag.'

'Well, today I felt like one and I didn't get the spins either.'

'So what did you do all day?'

'I went and saw a friend of my grandma's.'

'I didn't think you knew any.'

'I didn't until yesterday.'

'Evie, what are you crapping on about? Where did you get the, whatever it's called, board?'

'Al, can you meet me somewhere?'

'Now?'

'Yes, now.'

'It's nearly half past five and I've got to go to my dad's for dinner. He'll be here any minute. Mum's already meditating in the garage.'

'Can you ring me from your dad's place?'

'I'll try. It depends if the dickhead girlfriend spends the entire time on the phone. She usually does when I'm there.'

'Use your dad's mobile.'

'I said I'll try. Powell asked where you were.'

'That's because my assignment was due today.'

'I know. I told him your eye was still really bad. He looked mighty suss.'

'Tough tits.'

Evie hears the key in the front door. 'I better go. I think the liar from hell's home.'

'Who?'

'Who do you reckon?' Evie checks their bedside clock. 'And she's early, too.'

'I'll try and call you from Dad's.'

'Well, I mightn't be able to talk now.'

'I'll try and ring anyway.'

'Okay. See you.'

'Are you sure you're okay, Evie? You sound strange.'

Evie laughs. 'You know what, Alex? For the first time I don't feel it.' She hears her mother coming up the stairs. 'Better go. Bye.'

Robin comes in holding an armful of folders.

'What are you doing in my room?' she snaps.

'I was on the phone,' Evie snaps back.

She watches her mother's nose sniff the air. She knows what's coming next.

'Have you been smoking, Evie?'

She can't resist. 'No, Mum,' she answers innocently.

'Are you lying to me?'

'I don't know, mother. Are you?'

'I beg your pardon?'

'So you should be.'

Evie walks out of her parents' room. She is shaking. She knows she's stepping into uncharted territory. As she opens the door to her bedroom, it feels like everything is about to change. Behind her she can hear her mother's angry steps. They stop suddenly. The cupboard doors are open and the chair is still up against the drawers. Her mother is staring at something on the floor. Her forehead is wrinkling. Evie knows what she has seen. It sounds like a landslide crashing down a mountain. She grabs her cardigan and runs.

After nearly an hour of sitting in a park Evie goes home. Her dad is back from work. It's early for him. She stands by his car and looks at the house. From the outside it looks like any other evening but she knows now it's different in there. She can hear her mother yelling. Her dad is silent.

She nearly trips over a suitcase at the front door. The shouting stops.

'Evie?' she hears her dad call.

She walks into the kitchen. Her mother stands behind a

chair. Her grip is tight, like the wood could snap at any moment. Her father sits at the table with his head in his hands. When he looks up his face is pale. Evie thinks how old he looks. The ouija board is on the table.

'Where did you get this?' Her mother almost spits through clenched teeth.

Evie looks at her mother. In the park she made a decision. She's not going back. Why should the very essence of who she is be censored? She has denied, fought, hidden, and been petrified of herself. But today, just one day, has freed sixteen years of this incarceration. So Evie has decided she's not going back, back to who she was, ever again.

'Did you hear me?' she shouts. 'I said where did you get this bit of – witchcraft?'

'Robin! Stop it.'

'Well, what do you call it, Nick? Oh sorry, I forgot your mother called it a gift,' she shrieks, pacing over to him. 'Didn't she?'

'Don't speak about my mother like that. She's not here to defend herself.'

Robin's anger envelops the room like the rumbling of distant thunder before it claps and explodes.

'I can't do this any more, Nick,' her voice breaks. 'I just can't.'

She falls into the chair next to him and buries her head in his lap. Her sobs are loud and deep. His hands don't move from the table. It seems so much is lost between them. Evie looks at her crying, alone. Now she realises what the suitcase means. The massive consequences that Victoria predicted. She's sorry for her dad. About herself, she feels numb.

She goes up to her room and lies on the bed, listening to the words that understand her. 'Feel no shame for what you are, Feel no shame for what you are. Fall in light. Grow in light.'

The front door closes and a car pulls out of the driveway. The house is silent. She creeps down the stairs into the kitchen. It's empty. She tiptoes from room to room. There is no one left at home.

Evie takes a long, hot shower, washing away remnants of the old skin, cleansing the new. Her body feels warm and safe like it finally belongs to her. The doona swaddles her, the sheets are crisp and a sleep more peaceful than she's had in weeks welcomes her.

It's 5 a.m. when footsteps wake her. Someone is walking around the house. From the top of the stairs she sees a light on in the kitchen.

Nick is standing by the stove, waiting for the milk to boil.

'Dad?'

'Evie. I'm sorry, did I wake you?'

'She's gone?'

He nods.

'Where?'

'To Canberra to stay with Paula. She needs a break. She's a wreck.'

'Will she be away long?'

Nick hands her a cup of hot chocolate and shrugs. 'I don't know.'

'Dad, I have to explain what happened.'

'Only if you want to.'

'I do. Yesterday I wagged.'

'You wagged?'

'I went to see grandma's friend, Victoria. That's what I couldn't explain.'

Nick puts down his mug, spilling the hot drink onto the table.

'You see, she rang me.'

Evie tells him about the phone call and how she got the ouija board. He sits there quietly, nodding and frowning. It's almost like he's not surprised, just very tired. She knows it isn't the right time to tell him everything.

She goes back to bed and stares at the ceiling. She doesn't think about her visit to Victoria's or the girl's face and what it means. It's enough just to lie here listening to her breath, smelling her skin, absorbing who she is.

When her dad comes into her room he is shaved, showered and dressed in his Friday clothes, jeans and a black poloneck jumper. The eight o'clock news plays on the radio downstairs.

'I'm not going to school, Dad.'

Nick nods. 'I'll try and get home after lunch.'

'Okay.'

'Are you all right, Evie?'

'Are you?'

'I feel . . . sad,' he says. 'Sad that I couldn't make things different between you and your mother – all of us, really.'

'It's not your fault, Dad.'

'Let's just try and get through the weekend,' he says softly. 'I'm sure she'll phone.'

Evie feels her insides shrink as he turns and walks out. She has gained and he has lost. Pulling the doona over her head she tries to find that sleep again.

Evie dreams of being at a fair. She walks behind a man with dark hair. He is nearly as tall as her. He is leading her towards brightly coloured lights. They are in the shape of a star and go around and around. Watching it makes her giddy. She lifts her hand to her head and sees her sleeve is made of red silk. The cuffs are embroidered with black and gold flowers. She doesn't want to walk towards the lights but the man is holding her arm firmly.

The ground trembles and a loud noise rushes past her. It makes her trip. She looks down at silver lines running through the footpath. The black suede shoes she is wearing have a mark on the toe. Why can't they stop walking?

It's so dark and everyone's gone. She can't see where they're going. She falls against something and cuts her hand. It's a wire fence. She doesn't want to keep following him. She doesn't like him. He's not nice to her.

'Are you there?'
Alex's voice on the answering machine wakes her.
'Evie, are you there? Pick up the phone.'
She doesn't. Instead she records the dream in her book.
The next time the phone rings, it's her father's voice.
'It's Dad. Pick up the phone.'
She runs to answer it.

'Hi, Dad.'

'Did I wake you up?'

'No. I was just watching some TV.'

'Not the midday soaps?'

'How's your day?'

'It's busier than I expected. I won't be able to get home till about six.'

'That's okay. I'll see what's in the fridge.'

'Don't bother, let's have takeaway.'

'Okay.'

'What do you feel like? Japanese? Thai? Pizza?'

'How about Greek?'

'Greek?'

'Yep. I keep thinking about those yummy lamb kebabs. Theo'd be proud of me.'

'I'll bring some home from that place he takes us to.'

'Great, and some vine leaves, too.'

'Has Robin called?'

'No. Sorry.'

'Are you okay?'

'Yes.'

'I'll see you tonight. Bye.'

'Bye, Dad.'

They eat their takeaway straight from the plastic containers. No fancy table setting or good manners tonight.

Evie has eaten five vine leaves and is now up to her third

lamb kebab. She looks at her dad's plate. He's hardly touched his.

'Did you hear from Mum?'

'Paula rang as I was leaving the office.'

'Oh. How did she say Mum was?'

'Upset. Angry. With me, not you.'

'I'm sorry.'

'Evie, it's not your fault. Things have been bad between us for a while. We should've talked about it years ago.'

'But it's because of me.'

'Look, at the moment she can't handle things. It's just the way she is. The way she was brought up. I thought she'd change, that eventually she'd understand, but when I come to think of it, even years ago . . .' He buries his face in his hands. 'When, when. God.'

'What?' She lifts his fingers off his face, curling them around her own. 'When what, Dad?'

'You know, I haven't thought of it for so long and yet today it's all I could think of.'

'When what, Dad? Tell me!'

'When it saved you.'

'Saved me?'

'The Christmas you were two years old.' His voice wavers and he rubs his temples as he speaks. 'We were away. We stayed at these holiday flats up the coast. There was a swimming pool. One morning the phone rang; it was my mum. She said, 'Where's Evangaline?' She sounded in a panic. I gave the phone to Robin and went to look in your cot. You weren't there and the front door was open. I ran out, I was calling and calling you. Then Robin flew past me. I remember she kept screaming 'the pool, the pool'. There you were casually walking around the edge, like you were about to dive in and swim ten laps. We still don't know how you got out of the cot or the front door. Someone must have left the pool gate open.'

'And it was Grandma who told you?'

'Yes. She could see you standing at the edge of water. If she hadn't rung you probably would have fallen in and drowned. It was the most terrifying thing. We felt sick for weeks. I was so, so grateful to Mum and, and – her insight.'

Evie hears Victoria's words: *She should be thankful.* This is what she'd meant.

'Was Mum – thankful?'

'Darling, of course she was. But it freaked her out much more than I ever realised. She was a minister's daughter. She was taught to regard those things as wrong and evil. She couldn't help it. Looking back on it I was so naive. I thought what happened was maybe even a blessing in disguise, maybe the thing to make her think about it differently, be less paranoid. I was wrong. That should've been the point we started talking about the possibility of you being like – that.'

'But you didn't.'

'No. We didn't.' Her father hangs his head. 'You see, she wanted you to have a normal life. That's what was important to her, and when you began to show the tiniest sign of being like grandma, even though you were so little, it scared her. I think she felt bad she couldn't protect you, like she wasn't a good enough mother. Maybe that became her thing.'

'Protecting me? Controlling me, you mean?'

'I don't know. I thought things would be okay but that episode with Antonia Cipri, well, it was big, bigger than we imagined. I think she felt like it was out of control and she didn't want it –.'

'So if we didn't talk about it,' Evie blurts, 'then maybe we could pretend it wasn't happening? For me, Dad, that's what it's always been like.'

'I'm sorry, Evie. I should've taken the lead. I was the one that understood.'

'Dad? I think I should show you something.'

For a second Evie hesitates at the doorway of her bedroom. She understands this will be hard for him.

'Fantastic!' he says as she comes down with her art folder.

She passes just a few drawings to him, watching him admire them as though they're someone else's work.

'They're very good, Evie. Wow,' he squeezes her hand. 'This one looks like one of Theo's nieces. Who is it?'

'I don't know?'

He laughs. 'What do you –?'

But she catches his eye. She tries to make her look gentle. As he studies the portrait the confusion on his face transforms to recognition. 'Are you saying . . .'

She nods and looks away. She can't find any words of comfort.

'When? How long?'

'A while,' she whispers.

The weekend is quiet. Nick wants her to see their family doctor about her eye. He rings but they can't get an appointment until Monday. Evie is relieved; she doesn't feel like Dr Malouf's friendly chatter.

She tiptoes around the house. Her dad lies on the couch listening to music, reads every word in every newspaper and troubleshoots the phone calls from work.

'Damn, damn,' he shouts from the living room. She wonders if it's just the Sunday afternoon Rugby League. He hates it when the Wests Tigers get beaten.

'Evie?' he calls.

She stands at the doorway.

'Bloody Carla was meant to pick up some tapes from the police headquarters in Surry Hills,' he says, screwing up the newspapers strewn across the floor. 'She forgot and she's in Melbourne for the weekend. We need them for a story we're running tomorrow. I'm going to have to go in and get them.'

'I'll come with you.'

'Are you sure? I'm just going there and back.'

'I'll come for the drive.'

'Does that mean you're going to get out of your pyjamas?'

'I will if you will.'

Evie throws on a pair of cords and grabs her peacoat. She doesn't brush her hair. She hates feeling the sticky knot. It's getting bigger. It gives her the creeps.

They drive into town. The four o'clock news tells of

fighting in the Middle East, a flood somewhere in India, the proposed national budget and who's ahead in the golf. Evie thinks how removed these events are from her life. She makes up her own headlines. 'Teenage psychic's mother walks out.' Or 'Teenage psychic artist draws realistic pictures of people she's never seen before.'

Her dad is singing along with Bob Marley, 'No woman, No cry'. The words make Evie self-conscious. She stares out the window. Eye contact only makes it worse.

They drive into an underground carpark. A police officer in a security booth checks his journalist ID, ticking his name off a list.

'Who have you got there?' she winks.

'This is my daughter.'

She winks again. 'Haven't you got better things to do than drive around with your old man on a Sunday afternoon?' She seems to think this comment is hilarious.

Evie tries a laugh too but it doesn't come out right.

'Do you want to come up with me?'

'Well, I'm not staying in this spooky carpark with that nut.'

The lift opens into a sterile foyer. Their sandshoes squeak as they walk across the granite floor to the inquiry desk.

'Nick Simmons from Radio News,' he shows his ID again. 'I'm here to pick up some tapes from Detective Sergeant Brian Gould.'

'This way please, sir.'

'I won't be long, sweetheart.'

Her father disappears through an electronic security door. She sits on one of the grey flannel couches. There is nothing to read. The waiting room is empty. It's a quiet Sunday afternoon in the city.

She wanders around the foyer reading the notices alerting staff to security changes, positions vacant, social events and the upcoming Missing Persons Week.

Evie considers writing an advertisement for her mother. 'Robin Simmons. Last seen in Canberra. Stressed-out woman. Late forties, medium build.' She scans the missing persons poster to check she's following the right criteria. Name, date of birth, build, eyes, circumstances.

She is looking straight at her. Her face has become so familiar it takes Evie a while to register her photocopied presence here on the police station noticeboard. She looks and she reads but she isn't taking it in. Her father's voice is behind her.

'Okay,' he's saying. 'Let's go.'

She cannot move. Her body seems paralysed. She barely manages to lift her arm and point to the face.

'What's wrong?' His voice is bouncing off the granite floor. 'Evie?'

She feels him standing next to her. It takes all her strength to move her head to look at him. But he is staring at the poster, too.

'Evie?' he whispers. 'Oh god, Evie.'

PART
THREE

MISSING PERSONS

CAN YOU UNRAVEL THE MYSTERY?

ATHENA POULOS

DOB: 02/02/82
HAIR: Dark auburn
BUILD: Medium
EYES: Brown

CIRCUMSTANCES: Athena was last seen at West Terrace, Adelaide on 2 March 2002. She was living in Mile End with her family. It is believed she was headed for the Glendi Festival, Western Parklands. She has not contacted relatives since the date she went missing and there are grave concerns for her safety and welfare.

Report missing to: Keswick Police Station, SA
Missing Persons Unit Index No: AP56813740kh

'Can you unravel the mystery?' It's like a games show host shouting these words in Evie's head. She feels like she's losing her balance. She reaches out for her father's arm. Her throat feels tight. She's struggling to get a breath. Everything is going fuzzy. It's like a black curtain closing down on the set.

'Evie? Evie? Have a sip. It's okay. I'm here.'

She recognises the voice. She opens her eyes and sees her father's face.

'I'm here,' he says again.

'Dad?'

She is sitting on a cold, hard surface. Something is pushing into her back. She sees it's the same granite floor and a drinks machine behind her. She tries to stand up.

'We're still at the police station?'

'That's right. Put your arms around my neck.'

Her father sits her on the chair and holds a cup to her lips.

'Here, have some water.'

'Did I faint?'

'Nearly. I sort of caught you on the way down.' Some of her hair is falling into the cup. He takes it out and wraps it behind her ear. 'How are you feeling?'

'Can we go home, Dad?'

'Let's get you down to the car.'

'Okay.'

Her father puts his arm around her and slowly they walk to the lift. As the lift doors open he calls out something about a virus to the officer at the desk.

Nick brings her doona and pillow down to the couch. He sits with her feet on his knees. Evie wonders how they will start this conversation.

'I called Theo,' he says, wrapping the doona around her feet.

'How come?'

'Well, I'm not really sure how we should approach this.' Nick scratches his stubble. 'It could be a bit tricky.'

'She's from Adelaide, isn't she?'

'Yes. She has a Greek name. Theo has lots of contacts in Adelaide. He's the one who'll know where to start. I haven't a clue.'

'Why has this happened?'

'Evie, I wish I could give you an explanation.'

'I've never seen any of these people before, Dad. First it was Antonia's brother and now – her.'

He squeezes her foot. 'We're going to get through this. Okay?'

'What's her name?'

'Athena Poulos.'

'How old is she?'

'Twenty.'

'Did you say she was Greek?'

'Yes.'

'Remember you told me my drawing looked like one of Theo's nieces?'

'I do.'

'I'm really tired, Dad.'

'Close your eyes, sweetheart. I'll wake you when Theo gets here.'

'What time is it?'

'Ten to seven.'

'It's cold.'

'I'll get you another blanket.'

'Can you get my cardigan?'

Nick brings down her red cardigan. She slips it on and curls back under the doona.

'I'll be in the kitchen if you want me.'

Evie lifts her arm to her face, the soft wool stroking her chin. She runs the sleeve along her nose catching the smell of freshly mown grass. Burying her head in her arm, she whispers in the darkness, 'My red cardigan. My red cardigan's from Adelaide.'

Theo's voice is coming from the kitchen. Evie sits up and rubs her eyes. It feels late. Theo's reciting a list of names; he rolls them off with precision. 'Carl, Andy, Les Hargreaves, Deidre – the list goes on and on.'

'Who would you trust?' Nick's voice now.

'They're all pretty reliable but I guess I know Carl the best. Yeah, Carl'd be the one I'd trust the most.'

'I'd like to ring him tonight, Theo. She's okay at the moment but maybe it hasn't quite sunk in. I want to have something – positive to tell her.'

'Okay. He's in London but he should be able to pull some strings from there. You just tell me what you want me to do. Okay?'

'Thanks, mate.'

Theo's voice drops. 'What about Robin?'

'I don't know what to do there.' From the couch, Evie hears his voice is trembling. 'She doesn't know about this. God, Theo, I don't know how she'll take it.'

'Hey,' Theo is saying. 'We're going to get her through this. It's okay, buddy. I'll talk to her. Robin and I've always been able to talk.'

Silence.

'I should wake her up.'

Evie lies down and pretends to be asleep.

They're still sitting around the table at 2 a.m. Evie doubts any of them could sleep anyway. She has brought down the exercise book Victoria gave her and the portraits to show Theo. The horrible one, the one she drew last, is hidden in a drawer.

'Bloody hell! They're identical,' Theo shouts when he compares the missing persons leaflet with Evie's sketch. 'No wonder you fainted.'

They lean over her diary, reading it together. At first Evie feels self-conscious but the more they talk, the more she realises how seriously they're taking it.

The phone rings.

'That'll be Carl,' Theo says. 'It's 5 p.m. in London. I might take it upstairs.'

'No worries,' says Nick.

'Dad, I'd like to call Alex tomorrow. She's sort of in on it, too. I feel like I should tell her.'

'She's a good friend Alex. You've – no – *we've* been lucky to have her.'

'She's been so cool. I don't reckon there's many who could handle it like her.'

'How do you feel about calling Mum?'

'I'm not sure.' Evie knows this is something she has to confront. 'You know, in a funny kind of way I feel sorry for her. It's like I kind of understand that stuff with her father now. But she's not meant to be a part of this, Dad. I might call her tomorrow. I don't know.'

'I've got to ring her, Evie. I have to tell her about this. She's your mother.'

'I know, Dad. I'm just not ready to talk to her myself. Soon, maybe.'

Theo has finished on the phone. He sits back down and opens up his notebook. Evie and her mum tease Theo behind his back for being such a know-all.

'No wonder Corrina divorced him,' Robin would laugh. 'He'd drive you crazy. And that aftershave – it's a wonder he can breathe!'

'Okay, let's see,' Theo says, licking his fingers as he flips through the pages. 'I must say I picked the right man for the job. That was definitely worth the wait.'

Nick brings over fresh mugs of tea. 'So you got some facts for us?'

'I got facts,' he whistles.

'Theo? Did he, um – your friend – did he believe you?'

'Evie, he's over in the northern hemisphere and all the facts are here, in the southern hemisphere. He's been waking up people all over the country. Believe me, sweetheart, he wouldn't have taken off on a goose chase for nothing.'

'Okay,' nods Evie.

'I think we need to establish this early on.' Theo places his hands over Evie's knees and looks into her eyes. 'I believe you, and you know your dad believes you. These heavies in authority know me. They're not going to think I'm playing a bit of a trick.' He takes a long gulp of tea. 'Good cuppa, Nick. To be honest, we will run across sceptics. Maybe just a few, maybe a lot. But we know about this and we're used to it. We can't let it put us off. Remember, I knew your grandma, she was like my second mother. So I do know a bit about this.'

'Yep.'

'We, but especially you, honey, have to stay strong and focused. Me and your dad will be here but most of it's going to be on your shoulders and it might get tough.'

Nick frowns. Evie knows Theo's frankness worries him but she is grateful for it. They need someone like him.

'At first it seems the cops didn't suspect foul play,' Theo explains to them. 'You see, Athena had a proxy.'

'A what?' Evie asks.

'A potential husband. You know, an arranged marriage.'

'That's disgusting!'

Theo laughs. 'No, it's not. It actually works well for a lot of couples. My parents were an arranged marriage. They've been together nearly sixty years. Perhaps I should've had one?' He shakes his head. 'Nah, nothing could've saved Corrina and me.'

'But come on, Theo, I didn't think it'd still be done today.' Evie cringes. 'I mean, yuck, what if Athena didn't like the guy or already had a boyfriend?'

'Well, that seems to have been the problem. She *did* have a boyfriend and the family thought she'd run off with him. I get the impression Athena's parents must be fairly protective, in the traditional sense. Athena's boyfriend was a skip, not a Greek. She was completely against the guy her parents wanted her to marry and she'd been pretty rebellious in the past. So in the beginning, the family presumed she'd run off with the boyfriend and gone into hiding. They sent the family out to search for her. They reckon the cops described it like a military operation.'

'But she hasn't gone into hiding,' Evie says. 'Don't they realise that?'

'Well, now the boyfriend's been interviewed half a dozen times they do. He has a solid alibi and, according to the detective Carl spoke to, he's in a pretty bad way about the whole thing. It took a while for the family to tell the cops about the proxy arrangement and how the family network had been searching for her.'

The phone rings, then stops.

'That'll be the fax coming through. Can you get it, Nick?'

'So the police haven't been involved?' asks Evie.

'Well, no. Not until recently. Us Greeks like to do things our own way first.'

Nick scans the sheets as he separates them. 'Long fax,

seven pages. Looks pretty official, it's marked "strictly for addressee". It says none of the above agencies, Centrelink and so on, have been notified. Her bank account has not been accessed since the date of disappearance, blah, blah. And women's refuges and youth shelters have no record of her either.'

'Let's have a look.' Nick passes Theo half the pile of faxes. He shuffles through them. 'It says we have an appointment with CIB Detective Francis Cooper at 11 o'clock tomorrow.'

'We should all try and get some shut-eye. The sun'll be up in a few hours. Do you reckon you'll be able to sleep, Evie?'

'I'll try.'

'Good girl,' Theo says. 'You've always been a good girl. Maybe that's why you are who you are. Ever thought of that?'

Blushing, Evie shrugs.

'I mean, look at your old man. No wonder it bypassed him. Hey?'

'Yeah, yeah,' Nick replies.

They laugh. It's a relief for that moment, then Theo picks up a different picture of Athena and it's back to the reality.

'Notice anything?' he asks, holding it up like a teacher.

Nick and Evie take a look. 'No. What?'

'Have a closer look. She has what they call an identifiable feature.'

'I can't see anything, Theo.'

'Me neither,' says Nick. 'Tell us?'

'Athena's left eye is glass.'

Evie and her dad look at each other. Evie covers her left

eye with her hand. Nick opens his mouth but no words come out.

They step out of the lift and back onto the granite floor of police headquarters. Evie wears her tweed coat with the fur-lined collar, hoping it'll give her confidence or maybe give others confidence in her. Theo and she wait at the desk while Nick speaks to someone. Theo's hand is on her shoulder. His cologne floods the room.

'Come through,' a police officer says.

Theo squeezes Evie's shoulder as the electronic security door slides open. They are led down a corridor lined with TV monitors attached to the ceiling. A police officer opens a door marked Interview Room 3.

'Detectives Francis Cooper and Mary Thackeray will be with you in a moment,' she explains. 'Can I offer anyone tea or coffee?'

'Black coffee, thanks,' says Theo.

Evie sits at a table. There are three chairs on her side, two chairs on the other. The round clock on the wall reminds her of the one on *Play School*. It ticks loudly.

Nick comes in. 'You okay?' he says, sitting down and taking her hand in his.

She nods just as the doors burst open. The power and authority catch Evie off guard. She grabs hold of the desk before standing up.

A tall man with receding ginger hair holds out a large freckly hand. 'I'm Detective Francis Cooper, Evie. Call me

Frank, and this is Detective Sergeant Mary Thackeray.'

'Hello, Evie,' she says.

All Evie sees are her narrow eyes. She knows she isn't going to like this woman. Her head is already stuffed with doubt. Evie senses she's come along for the entertainment. She wishes she could tell her dad she doesn't want her here, but they have already started talking.

Evie finds her dad's hand under the table and holds it tight. Theo is explaining the situation like he knows it better than she does.

'Thank god for Theo,' Evie thinks, knowing her dad is thinking the same.

'The portrait is remarkable,' Frank says. 'How long ago did you draw it, Evie?'

Evie's fingers fumble with the pages of the exercise book.

'Um, June 12th is when I started drawing the first one. The other stuff kind of followed after that.'

'Have you seen missing persons posters before, Evie?' Mary of the narrow eyes asks this one.

'Um, I've seen those um, smaller ones at the video shop and newsagency and um, places like that.'

Mary mumbles something to Frank Cooper. 'I think we should check,' are the only words she says in an audible tone.

'I definitely haven't seen the poster of Athena before.' Evie interrupts. 'So there's no need to check.'

'Pardon?' responds narrow eyes.

Evie is using all her energy to intercept the detective's thoughts and it's exhausting. Theo and Nick give her a puzzled look.

'Nothing. Okay.' Evie shakes her head. 'Don't worry about it.' The old clay figures flash into her head. This time, she dismisses them. She smells a sceptic.

'Let's talk about the other things you've recorded. Like the dreams. Evie?'

'What?' Evie snaps at Detective Cooper. 'Sorry. Can you say that again?'

'The dreams. Tell me about them.'

Evie shuffles around in her chair and loosens the jumper around her neck.

'Um. The first one I had was really vivid,' she gulps. 'The girl in the dream had long hair. She was wearing a ring that had a red stone in the shape of a heart. She was trying to rip my red cardigan off me. There was this loud noise like bells or something. I don't know what it was. It was just really loud and sort of shook everything. I've heard the noise a couple of times now.'

Mary doesn't look like she's listening. She's busy laying out an enlarged missing person's poster on the table. She leans over Evie pointing to something in the picture.

'If you look closely. You can see Athena is wearing a chain around her neck. See?'

'It's got something on it,' Evie says, covering her bad eye. 'Look, I know what you're trying to say.'

'It's the love heart ring. See?'

'I just said, I know what you're trying to say.'

'Pardon?'

A bead of sweat sits on her top lip. It dribbles into her mouth.

'The other dream is of more interest to us,' continues Frank. 'Tell us about that one.'

'Yes. Tell us.' The narrow eyes watch and judge.

'I was – um – I was at a fair with this – um – this man.'

'Just take it slowly, Evie,' says Theo.

'Um – this man was walking towards these lights that were shaped like a star. They kept going around and around in circles.'

'Can you draw the star for me, Evie?'

'I think so.' She draws six radiating points of a star, like the one she remembers from her dream.

'And you're sure it was like this?' narrow eyes inquires.

Evie looks at Theo. 'I am sure.'

'You also mentioned a fence.' Frank flips through Evie's book. 'You say here, "My hand gets cut on a fence".'

'Yes.'

'Can you remember what the fence looked like?'

'I think so.'

'Can you draw it for me?'

Evie tries to picture the fence in the dream. There is something that identifies it but she can't get the detail right in her head. She's so distracted by the narrow eyes watching her every move. Her suspicious thoughts bore a hole through Evie's head like a jackhammer going off in her brain.

She begins to draw a line on the paper but her hands are shaking and sweaty. She's restless. There's not enough air in the room. She looks around at her dad.

'Take it slowly, darling,' he whispers. 'Just relax.'

'I can't!' She hears a thump. It's her fist on the table.

'What is it, Evie? Tell us, sweetheart.'

'Not with her here I can't!'

'Evie?'

'Make her go away, Dad,' Evie's voice growls. 'I can't concentrate with her here. She doesn't, she doesn't –'

'Doesn't what, Evie?' Theo is looking at her. 'Doesn't what?'

'She doesn't believe me! I can feel it.'

Evie's foot is tapping the floor. That and the ticking of the clock are too much. Evie jumps up and starts walking to the door.

'I've got to get out of here,' she is muttering. 'I can't breathe. Victoria told me to remove myself,' Evie points at Detective Sergeant Mary Thackeray. 'From people like *you*!'

Nick and Theo push their chairs aside and follow her out the door, down the corridor and to the lift. They almost have to jog to keep up. Evie pushes the 'G' button until the lift doors keep opening and closing. They're going nowhere.

'Evie?' Theo says. 'Evie? Stop it. Take a breath. Come on.'

She holds onto her dad's jumper. 'I'm sorry, I'm sorry. That woman, she was like . . .'

'Sshhh.' Her dad puts his arms around her. 'I'm not going to let anything bad happen to you. Ok? Theo and I are here.'

Evie's ribs hurt as she shakes and chokes. 'I don't know if I can do this, Dad.'

They go to a park across the road.

'Nick, I'll ring Frank and sort it out.' Theo paces up

and down. 'There's got to be something he can do. I mean, they wanted to see us.'

'Thanks, Theo.'

'Remember what I said, Evie. We're going to meet sceptics along the way and that's when you'll really have to keep your head together.'

'I just wasn't ready for that, Theo. She made me paranoid. I couldn't think straight.'

'Well, now you know what to expect if you encounter one.'

'It was like I had no energy. It was weird. I've never felt like that before not even with . . . Mum.'

'That's something else we really need to discuss,' Theo says under his breath. 'Nick?'

Nick puts his head in his hands and nods.

'But, let's get through this bit first. I'm going off in search of decent coffee. Who wants one?'

And with his mobile phone pressed to his ear, Theo crosses the road. He will make the necessary calls. He's good at that.

Evie links her arm through her dad's, puts her head on his shoulder and soaks up the sedating potion of the sun, a thought stuck in her head: she never felt like that with her mum. Not like with Mary of the narrow eyes. Never *that* bad!

Theo returns with a tray of takeaway cappuccinos, looking relieved.

'When you're ready, Evie, Frank'd like to see you back at headquarters. He promised Mary Dickface Thackeray won't be there.'

Evie laughs at Theo's description. Just his tone makes her feel lighter.

'Thanks, Theo.'

'He's very interested in what you have to say. He personally told me that.'

'I quite liked him,' Evie says. 'It was just her.'

'And the other big news is that I'm expecting a call from Athena's uncle.'

'What?'

'Don't underestimate us Greeks, Evie. We've got a real network, nationwide. It's not hard to track someone down. It just takes a few phone calls from your Uncle Theo.'

'Are you okay to go back?' asks Nick.

'I think so, Dad. I'm sorry, I didn't handle that well before.'

'I heard her tone too, Evie.'

'Okay, then,' Theo says. 'I'll call Frank and tell him we're on our way?'

Evie and her father look at each other and nod.

'Let's go,' Evie says.

They head back to police headquarters. Evie walks between her dad and Theo, her arms linked in theirs, her strength returning. This time it's the real thing.

'I'm sorry about before,' Frank says.

'That's okay.' Evie even manages a smile.

'I realise this must be very difficult for you. I've read through your diary carefully.' He holds up her exercise book. 'A lot of your detail corresponds with the case. Remarkable, really. There's enough to warrant me sending you to Adelaide. That's if you all agree, of course. I understand it's a very unusual situation.'

Evie's father puts his arms around her. 'It's up to you,' he says to Evie. 'Whatever you want to do, I'll support. Your call.'

'In the dream, you described the exact jacket Athena was wearing when she set off for the Glendi Festival,' Frank explains. 'Red silk with black and gold flowers. I'm also wondering if the fair you describe in the dream might even be the Glendi Festival? The Adelaide police had a couple of positive sightings to be fairly confident she did make it there.'

Evie, Nick and Theo sit forward in their seats.

'I've liaised with the South Australian police and spoken to one of the head CIB detectives. Now the Poulos family's communicating with them they feel there is probably a reason to suspect foul play, though they have no factual evidence of it. There's really very little to go on and the family is quite desperate. Everyone there agrees it's worth a shot you going over. There's nothing to lose except the taxpayers' money.'

'I'm expecting a call from a member of their family,' says Theo, getting out his notebook. 'An uncle. Con Poulos.'

Franks stands up and directs his words at the two men. 'Now, I have to say this. I don't want anything finding it's way to the media. We're dealing with a juvenile and the circumstances are very unusual. I'm sure it'd be a journo's dream stumbling across this type of story.'

'What are you suggesting?' Nick's anger is sudden and stinging. 'The last thing I want, or my daughter needs, is the press on our back. I'm standing on the other side of the fence this time. Look at me, I've got no power, no control. I know what they're like. I know what they'd do to her. How can you even –'

'It's okay, mate. It's okay,' Theo is saying. Theo, the middle-man this time.

The men discuss a media ban, the South Australian police, travel plans and adequate supervision. Evie watches Frank rub his chin and crack his knuckles, watches Theo wildly throw his arms around as he speaks and her dad frown and shake his head as he questions the potential dangers for his daughter.

But it's only her eyes that watch them. The rest of her feels and hears and smells and even tastes the cold and hollow loneliness of Athena Poulos. Now Evie knows.

'I want to go to Adelaide,' she announces.

The men stop and look at her. 'Okay,' they say.

Their plane has been delayed half an hour. They sit in the business lounge waiting. Theo eats the small triangular sandwiches and Nick drinks the coffee, even though he keeps saying how bad it is. Evie fiddles with her discman.

'So what did Dr Malouf say about Evie's eye?' Theo speaks through a mouthful of curried egg.

'That reminds me,' Nick says. 'Time for your eye medicine.'

He hands her a bag containing two types of eye drops and a thin tube of ointment.

'What did he give her?'

'Some antibiotics and anti-inflammatory cream.'

'So what did he say it was?'

'He thinks it's uveitis, some eye infection.'

'How do you spell it?'

'I don't know, Theo. U-v-e-i-t-i-s, I s'pose?'

'And how do you get it?'

'Why are you writing this down, mate? You've gone deadset mad with that notebook.'

'I just reckon we should be informed about this. Don't you, Evie?'

'You two sound like a couple of old women,' laughs Evie. She enjoys their banter. 'Actually, Dad, I do think it's a good idea. Victoria said I should record everything, just in case.'

'There we go, even your daughter and the mysterious Victoria agree with me,' Theo says. 'Now, how did the good doctor say you get it?'

'I'll tell him, Dad,' she teases. 'He thinks a while ago I probably got something in my eye and it didn't all come out. He called it a retained foreign body! I'll never forget that line.'

'You put the drops in both eyes?'

'Apparently it can easily spread to the other eye. I'd be really attractive then, wouldn't I?' Evie slips on her new sunglasses. 'Do you like them, Theo?'

'They're pretty cool.'

'So they should be,' Nick interrupts. 'They cost me a bloody fortune. I can't believe I bought my sixteen-year-old daughter Gucci sunglasses.'

'It's the stress, mate,' Theo laughs.

Nick gives him a look. Theo pulls a funny face. These are the moments Evie craves – light, silly, flippant.

'Flight Q1-11 to Adelaide is now ready for boarding. Please have your boarding passes ready.' The announcement echoes through the lounge.

Nick holds out his hand to his daughter. 'That's us.'

'It's time,' Evie sighs, wrapping his hand around her shoulder.

'You okay?' he asks softly.

'You know, Dad, I can't get there quick enough. That's the truth. I want to get this over and done with.'

Evie feels self-conscious walking down the aisle, looking for her seat. She senses the other passengers staring at her. Wearing her tweed coat and high camel boots, her long beaded earrings and Gucci sunglasses, she can guess what they think about the stylish girl who looks older than her years. How easily the outer shell fools, she thinks.

Evie grips the seat as they take off and lift through the cloud cover.

Ding, the seatbelt sign turns off. The plane seems motionless as it glides above the still, blue landscape. Evie stares out the window. Athena is dead. The knowledge sits in her bones.

'Maybe you knew her in a past life?' Alex said on the phone last night.

'Maybe,' Evie had answered.

'Maybe she was your best friend in a past life?'

Evie gets out her sketchbook. She isn't going to do any

drawings, at least not for a while. She turns to a blank page. Her dad and Theo sit a couple of rows ahead. This is why she wanted to be on her own; there are things she needs to say. Things she needs to ask.

Dear Athena,

Today is Wednesday 5th July and I'm on my way to Adelaide to meet your family. I hope I can do what you've sent me here for. It feels strange and I'm scared because I don't really know what to expect. But if you're with me then I won't feel so alone and that's probably what I'm most scared of.

When I think about how alone you were at the end it makes me feel emptier than I ever could have thought possible. It's like a hole in my chest, a hollowness in my gut and a feeling of such dread I feel like I can't breathe. I've had this feeling before, but not like this. It's so powerful. It's horrible. I hate it. I'd do anything to make it go away and that's probably why I'm here. I don't mean that to sound selfish.

Please show me what to do because I haven't a clue and I know people are counting on me (especially Dad and Theo). I used to push these weird feelings away, thinking they'd give up and leave me alone. But now I understand it's not like that. So, I'll let you into my heart and head and do everything I can to help your family put you to rest. Then will you leave me alone? 'Cause I think I'm starting to realise I need to put some things to rest in my own family, too, and I can't do both at the same time.

I hope that doesn't sound rude, as heaps of good things have come out of this. I've grown up a lot the past few days. It's been big. At last I'm beginning to understand about myself and my gift (I feel stupid calling it that). I don't have to sneak around pretending nothing's going on, and now I have people I can talk to. I never had that before. If it wasn't for you I wouldn't have met Victoria.

I shouldn't whinge. I'm alive.

Things are stuffed with my mother, at least that's how it feels, and yet I reckon all of this has actually made me understand her a bit more. I really don't think she can help it. She's scared, and if you ask my opinion I reckon it was her father who made her like that. He died before I was born and Mum doesn't talk about him much but when she does she gets this look in her eyes. It's sort of sad and frightened. I think that was the way she looked just before she left (although I can't remember clearly, that whole night's a bit of a blur). That's the other thing I'm beginning to understand: we are who we are.

My friend Alex reckons she's been waiting for this to happen. She said, 'Well, Evie, it sounds like the shit finally hit the fan.' And I said, 'No, Alex, it was more like a monster turd collided with a windmill.' We had a good laugh after that except then she started crying and I did, too. Mum and I probably just need some time apart. Alex thinks maybe I knew you in a past life. She's always been into that stuff even though she hadn't heard of a ouija board. Dag!

Anyway, my dad keeps turning around and looking at me

so I better go. If he sees me writing this he'll really think I've flipped. Poor Dad.

Love, Evie xxxxx

P.S. In some ways I feel like I should be saying thank you. I just hope you'll be able to thank me, too. E xo

The minute they walk into the arrivals lounge Evie notices them. Two big men in navy suits.

Theo nudges her. 'See those two suits over there,' he says with a wink. 'That'll be them.'

'Mr Simmons?' The older one holds out his hand to Theo.

Theo points behind him.

'Oh? Mr Simmons?' He shakes hands with Nick. 'Senior Detective Vic Spry, South Australian Police.'

'How do you do,' says Nick. 'This is my colleague and close friend Theo Kavlakis and this is my daughter, Evie.'

The detective looks at Evie and smiles. His face looks kind but his eyes are weary.

'Hello.' Evie holds his hand firmly.

'How was your flight?'

'Fine, thank you.'

They walk towards the other suit.

'Evie, this is Detective Sergeant Rory Van de Meer. He is my partner on the case.'

'Hello,' Evie says.

He is young and fresh. He hasn't seen too much, yet.

'How was your flight?' he asks.

'Fine, thank you,' Evie answers again.

They walk out to the white Holden Commodore that is conveniently parked in the 'no stopping' zone. They load the bags into the boot.

'Have you been to Adelaide before, Evie?'

'No, I haven't, Detective, um . . .'

'Call me Rory,' he smiles.

'Okay.' Evie notices his teeth. They are thick, capped and very straight, revealing his need for perfection.

Theo, Nick and Evie squash into the back seat.

'We've got you booked into the Hilton.' Detective Vic Spry starts the housekeeping conversation. 'It's a convenient spot, close to police headquarters and the Mile End area. Actually, we'll drive through Mile End on our way in.'

'We'll pass where the Glendi Festival's held, too,' says Rory from behind the wheel. 'Tell us if you want us to stop anywhere.'

'Is there something there now?' asks Nick.

'No,' answers Rory. 'It's just parkland. The festival only goes for one weekend.'

'I know all about the festival,' Theo says. 'It's a celebration of Greek independence from the Turks.'

Theo launches into a history lecture on Greek–Turkish relations. Evie's sure the two detectives are rolling their eyeballs.

Nick winds down the window. 'What else is at Mile End?' he asks.

'There's a big railway terminal,' replies Vic. 'It's where the Ghan, the Overland and the Indian Pacific meet.'

'It's the Keswick Terminal.' Rory adds in the extras. 'There's a goods line and a passenger line.'

'Really?' Nick nods.

Evie isn't really following their conversation. It's that uncomfortable trying-to-break-the-ice, get-to-know-you kind of talk she'd rather avoid. Who cares what's there? she thinks. She's here to help Athena, not make boring small talk.

'It's stuffy,' Evie says, slipping her shoulders out of the tweed coat.

'Theo, wind down your window, mate,' Nick says.

Evie pulls open her jumper and blows into the neck. 'I'm so hot.'

'Here,' Theo says, helping her with her coat. 'Give me that and take your jumper off.'

'I hope you're not getting sick,' Nick sighs.

She senses the detectives exchange a look.

'Stop the car,' she calls, surprising herself as much as the others.

'What is it?' asks Nick.

'We're here, aren't we?' Evie says to them. She leans over her father and looks out the window. 'This is where the festival's held, isn't it?'

Rory turns around. 'Do you want to get out?'

'I'm so hot.' She pulls at her seatbelt. 'I want to get something out of the boot.'

'What is it, Evie?'

'It's just something I need, Dad,' she snaps. 'God, I'm suffocating in here.'

She can't undo the belt. The clasp is stuck. She tugs at it.

'I can't believe I forgot it,' she keeps muttering. 'I can't believe it. Can someone let me out of this car? I can't, can't – breathe!'

Evie rips the belt off, fighting her way out of the car. She leans over the boot shaking, trying to get her breath.

'Get someone to open the boot, Dad.'

Rory presses the magic button and the boot pops open.

Evie pulls her bag out and starts rummaging through it. 'I know I packed it,' she says over and over. 'I did. I know I did.'

Nick, Theo and the detectives stand back, watching her. She is almost chucking things out of her bag. Things she wouldn't normally like strangers to see – bras, undies, tights, a packet of panty liners.

'Got it!'

She opens the lid of a small black box and slips the square-shaped silver bangle over her wrist. The comfort wraps around her like the softest woollen blanket.

The men still watch in silence.

'My mother's bangle?' Nick stammers.

Evie shrugs. She knows to them she looks crazy, yet she doesn't care and even that feels strange.

'Do you want to have a walk around?' Rory finally says, back to business.

'Okay,' says Evie. 'Do you mind if I go by myself?'

'We'll wait here,' he replies. 'Give us a yell if you need anything.'

Evie wanders around the park. She can see the men standing by the car. Vic's smoking and Theo and Rory are chatting. Her dad hasn't taken his eyes off her.

A jumbled sound drifts towards her. Every now and then it gets a little louder. Evie walks towards it. It's so close now. Music, screaming, laughter; it's just for her ears. 'Does the festival have rides?' she calls.

Rory comes over to where she's standing. 'They have a merry-go-round, dodgem cars, a ferris wheel –'

Suddenly she interrupts. 'There's the star!' Evie is pointing to the air.

Rory looks up.

'It's so big,' she gasps. 'The star's all lit up. It's going around and around.'

In her mind's eye she can see the back of Athena, her long, dark hair falling behind her as she walks towards the star. Evie follows her through the noise.

'Oh, she doesn't want to go on it.' There's a whining sound to her voice. Evie reaches out her hand. 'No. Don't. Stop it! He's taking her hand. He's making her. He says she has to. He says she's chicken.'

The others have joined them. Vic holds a small recorder.

'Stop, she doesn't want to!' Evie cries out, twisting the bangle around and around her wrist. 'She hates the ferris wheel.'

Evie stops. Athena's gone. The men are standing around, watching her. She presses her lips together, her face flushing.

'She came here with someone she didn't like.' Evie looks down, digging her toe into the dirt. They're still staring at her. 'Someone who made her go on the ferris wheel. She must've tried to get away after that.'

'Where did she go, Evie?'

She frowns at Rory. 'I don't know.'

They check into the hotel.

'That's bloody generous of them,' grumbles Theo, as the porter unlocks one hotel room with two double beds. 'Any chance of another room, mate?'

'There's an adjoining room,' Evie giggles.

She's sure Theo's one of those men who take hours in the bathroom. He's holding the most enormous toiletries bag. She catches a look from her dad and tries to suppress the laugh that's sitting in her throat.

'What's so funny?' Theo asks.

'You're cute, Theo.'

'Why? What'd I do?'

'Nothing!'

'Are you trying to read my mind, Evangaline Simmons?'

They hang around the room. Theo orders a club sandwich and takes a beer from the mini bar. Evie lies on the bed listening to her discman, and Nick stares out the window, an open book in his lap.

'Well, no use just sitting around.' Theo drains the last drop from the bottle. 'I might go and check out the gym. Anyone interested?'

'You go,' Nick says. 'I'm expecting a call from Robin.'

'Come on. Twenty minutes on the treadmill will do you good.'

'I'm fine, mate.'

But when Theo's mobile rings Nick jumps.

'Theo Kavlakis? Yes, hello. Thank you, it was fine. I'm so sorry.' He starts speaking softly in Greek then calls out in

English. 'That's amazing! I will. Thank you. Yes. I'll tell her. We'll see you soon.'

'Well?'

Evie and Nick stand there waiting for the news.

'That was Athena's uncle,' begins Theo. 'They just spoke to Vic and Rory. The ferris wheel at the Glendi Festival is famous for its fairy-lights display. Each year the lights are hung in a different pattern. This year it was a six-pronged star.'

Evie drops onto the bed, the saliva pooling in her mouth.

Theo keeps talking. 'Athena was terrified of the ferris wheel. She hated any sort of heights. When she first disappeared, the police had a report that someone saw her on the ferris wheel, crying. Her family said no way it would've been her, she'd never, ever go on it, it was a real phobia. So the police disregarded it as a false sighting but of course the family remembered the report. They're very excited about meeting you. It means a lot to them.'

'Theo?' whispers Evie, her fingers holding her throat. 'We're not going to find her alive.'

He slumps down next to her. 'Are you sure?'

She nods. They sit in silence.

'Are you going to tell the police?'

'I'm sure they already think that. They're looking for a body. They want to close the case. The missing persons case, that is.'

They drive through Adelaide bound for the western suburb of Mile End. It is time to meet the family.

'How flat is this place,' notices Evie, as she watches the suburbs pass by. 'Flat, flat, flat, flat as a pancake,' the words start in her head. 'Flat as a pancake, flat as a pancake.' They gather rhythm and momentum. 'Flat, flat, flat. Flat as a pancake. Flat as a pancake. Flat as a railway track.' The voice in her head grows louder. 'Flat as a railway track, flat as a railway track, flat as a railway track.'

A shrieking sound races past, all bells and thundering. It's the sound from her dream. The tyres bump and rattle over a railway crossing. Evie wipes her hands on her jeans and swallows hard.

The Poulos house stands in a quiet street. A bull-nosed tin roof covers the front entrance. The door is open. They have been waiting for her. Theo and the detectives go in first. Evie waits in the car with her father.

'You're being really brave, Evie.'

'This has been the longest day of my life. There's a circus going on up here.' She points to her head. 'And it's getting harder to ignore.'

Nick frowns. His hair sticks up at the front, reminding her of a little boy, dazed, just woken from sleep.

'I don't really know what I'm doing, Dad.'

He reaches out and touches her cheek.

'What am I meant to do? Just go in?'

'You'll be great.'

She points to the house. 'I'm petrified. I think this is the bit I've been dreading the most. How am I going to look them in the face? What can I say to them? I . . . I don't know what I can –?'

'Just be yourself, Evie.'

Theo calls them.

'Okay?'

Evie nods. As Nick steps out of the car she notices he's wearing odd socks. Evie's leg's tremble as they walk up the stairs to the front door. She grabs her father's hand. He steadies her.

At the entrance stands a small woman dressed in black. Next to her is a stocky man with a bushy beard flecked with grey. He wears a black armband over his jumper. The lady puts her arms around Evie and holds her for a moment. The man does the same. When he steps back, Evie sees that he is crying.

'Thank you for coming,' the lady whispers. Her pale skin makes the dark circles under her eyes look painted. They follow the couple down a narrow hallway to a large room. There are people sitting around also dressed in black. All the men look unshaven and wear the same black armbands.

Evie takes off her coat and sunglasses. Athena's mother pats the seat next to her.

'Come and sit,' she says.

As Evie walks over to the couch the mother gasps and starts speaking in Greek. Evie looks at Theo for a translation but he has joined in the frantic conversation.

The words are mixed in Greek and English. Everyone is talking loudly and pointing to their face. She can't understand what they're saying. Again, she looks at Theo.

'It's your eye,' he tells her. 'They're saying it's the same as Athena's.'

Evie covers her left eye. She doesn't understand what they mean.

A girl Evie hasn't seen steps out from behind a door.

'My sister had an eye condition,' she explains quietly. 'It started after she got a splinter in her eye. She had to have a glass eye fitted. My parents think you have that, too.'

'A glass eye?'

'No. The same thing before she got the glass eye. The doctor called it uveitis. It was the left eye, too.'

The bile rises in Evie's throat. She tastes its bitterness. Covering her mouth she stumbles down the hall, searching for the bathroom. The girl runs after her.

Evie's stands over the toilet vomiting hard and loud but there is no relief.

'Are you all right?' the girl asks.

'Huh?'

Wedged between the toilet and the basin Evie looks up at the girl. She is like Athena only younger.

'Evie?' her father is at the door too. 'Are you okay?'

She nods. 'Just, just give us a minute, Dad.'

He stands there looking down at her, then walks away.

The girl takes Evie's arm and helps her off the floor. Evie leans against the tiled wall.

'I'm Melena,' the girl says. 'Athena's little sister. Well, only sister actually.'

Athena's mother comes to the doorway.

'Can I get you something, Evie?'

'She's okay, Mamma.'

'I'll . . . I'll just stay here for a minute, Mrs Poulos. I'll be fine in a sec.'

When Athena's mother leaves Melena whispers, 'Do you know what happened to my sister?'

'I'm not sure. I'm trying.'

'She didn't want to go to the Glendi Festival,' Melena continues. 'She wanted to go to a dance party with Pete. That's her boyfriend.'

'But she did go to the festival.'

'I know. They made her go.' Now Melena speaks so softly it's hard to hear. 'They had arranged for her to go with Yannis. He's the guy she was meant to marry but she didn't want to.'

'Is he out there?' Evie gestures out to the living room.

'No. He's back in Greece. He said he was insulted.'

'Did you like him?'

'Not really. He was very, you know, traditional. Thena wasn't into all of that.'

'Did you say Thena?'

'That's what the family call her.'

Evie grabs hold of the basin swallowing back the air.

'Are you going to be sick again?'

'Melena?' her mother calls. She says something else in Greek.

'We better go back out there,' she says. 'My mother's getting impatient. She wants to know everything you see. Are you sure you're okay? This is all pretty weird.'

Evie rinses her mouth and splashes her face, careful to avoid the mirror. She stands over the basin for an extra second.

'Okay,' she says. 'I'm ready.'

Mrs Poulos nurses a photo album on her lap. 'Would you like to see some pictures? Come and sit with me. Let me show you my little Athena.'

Evie sits there trying to swallow, breathe, appear calm and interested all at the same time and it's hard. To her it's like watching the whole thing on a TV in another lounge room in another house. Her body's present but that's about it.

'This is my favourite one of little Thena,' she says, passing Evie the album. 'She looks so sweet in her red cardigan.'

Evie stares at the photo of a girl with dark curls sitting on a swing. The chubby fingers are playing with the buttons on her cardigan. Covering her left eye Evie leans over, taking a closer look at the little blue dots that are shaped like teddies. The bile rises in her throat again, bitter and stinging. Evie pushes the album away and staggers over to her father, throwing her arms around him.

'Daaaddy. Oooh, Daaaaddy.' And from the very pit of her stomach rises a cry that echoes through the room.

They take her back to the hotel. She has had enough.

'We'll need Evie to come up to headquarters at some time. There's paperwork we have to do.' Vic Spry is back to house-keeping. 'We'll call in the morning.'

Evie hears the conversation around her. She's too exhausted to talk. Her brain has shut down as though it can't take in any more or doesn't want to. Crawling into bed, disappearing into a mindless sleep only possible after those many tears, is all she can do.

'Are you sure she doesn't want to talk to anyone?' asks Rory. 'The victim support service could easily send someone over to the hotel. She wouldn't have to come into the station.'

'I just want to get her inside,' Nick says.

They walk up the stairs to the hotel's entrance. A hand gently holds her elbow. It's Theo. Her father is still outside the glass doors talking to the police.

'You're going good, honey,' he says, steering her towards the lift. 'Let's get you upstairs.'

A layer of sweat shines on Theo's forehead. His dark bushy eyebrows sit low on his forehead in a permanent frown but what Evie notices most is the first real whiff of his true body odour, and it makes her think of her mother.

Evie sleeps till after dusk. A night sky sprinkled with stars shines through their hotel window. Theo is snoring in the adjoining room and the rattle of cutlery echoes as her dad stacks up the room service trays. She feels the corner of her sketchpad under the pillow.

'Are you sure you won't eat anything, sweetheart?'

'I'm not hungry, Dad.'

'Does your tummy feel a bit more normal?'

'I don't reckon it'll feel normal until we're out of here.' What Evie really wants to say is 'What's normal?'

'I'm going to bed. Theo and I've got a teleconference set up downstairs for the morning. It's just a production meeting, it shouldn't take long.'

'What time?'

'Eight forty-five. Are you still thinking of going to the art gallery?'

'Maybe.'

He sits on her bed. 'I'm sure this'll be over soon.'

'I hope so.' She can barely lift the corners of her mouth.

'I spoke to your mum.'

'Yeah?'

'She said what a good job you're doing. She said losing a daughter would be the worst thing imaginable.'

'Really?'

'She said she'd like to hear your voice.'

'Yeah?'

'I said you might call her tomorrow. You could tell her about the Dobell exhibition if you go to the gallery. She'd love to hear about that. She's always been so proud of the way you draw.'

'I get it from her.'

'So you do.' He strokes her forehead. 'I was proud of you today. That was, well, about the hardest thing I've ever witnessed.'

'Dad? Mum's mother drew, too, didn't she?'

'She did.'

'I remember Mum once told me she had some drawings of hers.'

'They're sketches of Robin. I've only seen them once or twice. They're very good.'

'She must have been very little when they were done.'

'Three or four, I'd say.'

'Mum was four when she died?'

'Five. Just five.'

'Do you think Mum will let me have the drawings one day?'

'I don't think she'd want anyone else to have them.'

Evie blows him a gentle kiss. 'Goodnight, Dad.'

The single light from Evie's lamp shines over her bed. Under the pillow she reaches for her sketchpad and opens to the letter she wrote on the plane. Ruling a line underneath she begins a new one.

Dear Athena,

This afternoon I met your sister, Melena. I know she really misses you. I could feel her emptiness. Your dad didn't say much. Your mum showed me photos of you as a kid. That completely blew me out – if it's actually possible for me to be any more blown out. How did that happen? I don't reckon anyone could explain that. Do you? It's creepy! Is this why it's happened? I wish I knew.

My dad reminded me of it a couple of months ago and even then I could only just remember. My imaginary friend, Thena, the little girl whose claim to fame was a red cardigan with blue teddy buttons. They probably reckoned it was some sneaky way of me trying to get a cute cardigan. But you were true. I haven't spoken to Mum for nearly six days. My dad has. He says she wants to hear my voice. Do you think she does? She said I'm doing a good job.

There is something I'm beginning to understand. The cardigan I wear to school, the same one I drew your portrait in and the one I wore when my left eye started to blur, the cardigan that Dad bought me in Adelaide. That's your cardigan – your red cardigan.

I'll wear it now, while I'm here. There's still a part of you in it. Once I found a tiny knot of hair in one of the seams. It was yours, wasn't it?

Please help me because I want to go home.

Love, Evie

P.S. It's still Wednesday 5th July. The longest day in my life – ever!

P.P.S. If I wear your cardi and my grandma's bangle, something's got to happen or I'm out of business.

The next morning, Evie meets her dad in the lobby. He's just finished his teleconference. His hair is combed and his walk confident.

'How did you sleep?' he asks.

'I only woke up half an hour ago.'

'You needed it. Did you have some breakfast?'

'Yes,' answers Evie, not letting her dad know a cup of coffee is her definition of breakfast today.

'Here's my mobile phone and here's Theo's mobile number. I wish you'd let me get you one.'

'Dad, I know I'm probably the only teenager without a mobile but I hate them. You know that.'

'Well, you're having this today, no argument, young lady.'

'Yes, sir.'

'You seem a bit brighter.'

'So do you, actually.'

'Really?'

'Today I'm working on tricking myself,' she says. 'I'm convinced it's going to be a good day. I'm hanging to go home, Dad.'

'I know, darling,' he soothes, buttoning up her coat. 'We have to go to police headquarters today.'

'Detective Vic has called already?'

'Twice.'

'So what time?'

'He said about midday.'

'All right.'

'What are we going to do about your eye, Evie?'

'It'll be fine, Dad. I'm not going to end up with a glass one, I can tell you that!'

'Okay,' he laughs. 'I'm heading down to the park – clear my head. Do you want me to meet you at the art gallery later?'

'No,' Evie says. 'I'll meet you at the police station. I've got a map.'

'Are you sure you'll be okay?'

'Yes. I feel like a quiet morning cruising the gallery. It'll be good for me. I need the space. It might help me clear my head too.'

'Use the mobile to ring Mum – if you want. You could give her a live commentary as you walk through the exhibition. She'd like that.'

'Maybe.'

'And ring me if you need me. Promise?'

'Promise, Dad.'

She walks him to the junction of King William and

Carrington Streets, kisses him goodbye and waits for him to turn the corner. Then she slips her coat off, takes the red cardigan out of her bag and puts it on. She does the buttons up, shines her bangle on the cuff, puts her coat back on and walks back towards the gallery.

She doesn't want her dad to know about the cardigan. The guilt he's carried all these years is enough. Evie wants him to just consider it a gift that he gave her – a gift that she loves. And that's how she'll leave it.

She takes out the mobile and dials Alex's number. That's an easy call. Thursday is her late morning and Evie crosses her fingers as she hears someone pick up.

'Hello.'

'Al!'

'Evie? Evie, is that you? Are you home?'

'No. God, I miss you.'

'I miss you, too. How's it going?'

Evie goes to tell but changes her mind. 'No, tell me about you. What's happening at home?'

'Um? You've only been away a couple of days, Evie.'

'I don't care,' Evie whines. 'Tell me anything. The stupidest, dumbest things. Anything!'

'Let's see. It's raining. Um?'

'It's freezing here.'

An icy wind whistles. Rubbish blows out of a bin and scuttles along the gutter.

'Here's a bit of goss. Poppy's back and had a bit of a Gold Coast romance.'

'Oh my god, that is a bit of goss! Who was it?'

'Some guy at the wedding called Angus. He's already called her.'

'Is she happy?'

'Can't wipe the smile off her face. Of course she's being very secretive about what actually went on between them.'

'Has anyone noticed I'm not at school?'

'Just Poppy obviously.'

'What did you say?'

'I told her some bullshit about a great-aunt's funeral.'

'Has she seen Seb?'

'Actually she made a joke about him being quiet on the bus yesterday. I haven't told her anything. I promise,' adds Alex.

'I know you won't say anything. I didn't mean it like that. I keep thinking about how weird it's going to be seeing Seb again. Well, I'm thinking about that along with about ten thousand other things.'

'Are you hanging in there, girlfriend?'

'Just.'

A newspaper board clatters along the footpath. Evie tries to decipher the headlines as it somersaults in front of her.

'So what's Adelaide like?'

'I'm hardly sightseeing.'

'Sorry. I keep saying the wrong things.'

'No, you don't. I don't even know why I asked you about school. I honestly don't care.'

'You don't?'

'No. I mean, I guess there's stuff – shit!' Evie says, almost tripping over the newspaper board.

'What?'

'Nothing. I just nearly broke my neck.' Looping her hand through the wire edge, Evie picks up the board and leans it against a shop window. Like a slap across the face, she suddenly realises what it was about the wire fence in her dream. What she couldn't recall with the narrow-eyed detective in Sydney now jumps up and down in front of her.

'Al, I've got to go.'

Evie gets out her exercise book. Resting it against a window she begins to write but her hand, in defiance of her head, draws instead. Her wrist has a mind of its own, flicking up, down and in circular sweeps. Quickly she looks around; no one has noticed.

She recognises it immediately. This is the fence from her dream. Running along the top are barbed wire circles interlinked with one another. She holds the drawing on different angles, searching for another clue.

There's a scratch in the curve of her hand where her thumb and index finger meet. It wasn't there before. She turns her hand over. Hundreds of tiny scratch marks cover her palm, climb up her fingers over to the other side. Blood is smudged on the side of the page. She looks at her other hand – it's the same. She drops the book, hiding her hands behind her back. She's gasping. She can't get a breath. Her throat is so tight. There's no air.

The exercise book, her diary, is lying on the footpath. She has to pick it up but everything is moving, swaying. Her fingers fumble for the mobile in her bag but they shake so much it takes five attempts to press the right buttons. There's blood smeared over the numbers, over the back of the phone.

She hears him, 'Theo Kavlakis,' but her vocal cords are paralysed. She can only mouth at the air.

'Evie? Evie is that you?' he calls. 'Nick? Nick, I think it's Evie.'

'Evie?'

'D-Daaad? Dad? Come and get me, now!'

'Evie, tell me where you are!'

'Um, um I don't know, I don't know, I – I?'

'Can you see a street sign?'

'No, no. I'm just, um, just near where . . . where we said goodbye.'

'Evie, stay where you are. Don't move. We're coming. Okay?'

'Dad?' she moans. 'My hands, my hands.'

Evie stumbles up and down the block. People push past her, giving her strange looks as she gets in their way. She can't help it. It's as though she's lost her sense of balance. Noise is bouncing off the buildings, colliding in her head. Her hands sit in the pockets of her coat. She can't look at them. She doesn't understand.

Wasn't she just chatting to Alex on the phone? She wants to be talking to Alex again. She wants to go home. Somewhere. Anywhere. She wants it to stop – stop right now!

Her father's hand is firm on her back. He is guiding her through the pedestrian traffic and into a taxi. Theo leans over and helps with her seatbelt. He tries to move her arm.

'No. No. Don't,' Evie screams.

The taxi driver jumps out of his cab shouting, 'What the bloody hell's going on? Get out of my cab.'

Theo gets out, too. He's saying something to the driver,

trying to calm him down. 'We have to get to the police headquarters, Angas Street. Please, mate.'

Evie is just aware of someone touching her arm, steering
her through double glass doors. She watches her shoes walk
down a thick carpeted corridor, one foot in front of the other,
the sponginess bouncing off her soles. It's like walking on the
moon.

She is guided into a chair. Vic and Rory are standing there.
Her father and Theo, too.

'Take it slowly,' Vic is saying to her. 'Take some deep
breaths. You're safe here.'

'The fence,' she hears her voice echo. 'The fence.'

Slowly she lifts her hands out of the pockets and sits them
on the table palms facing up.

'Shit!' her dad yells.

Shaking her head she hides them back in her coat.

The men huddle around whispering. A phone rings,
muffled voices, the smell of coffee, doors opening and
closing but Evie sits aloof, detached from the physical world.

Instead she sits there aware of a strange calmness entering
her body. Evie feels it break through her skin and settle in the
deepest layer. It quietens her mind, taking the edge off her
fear. She knows why. Fear will only be in the way now. She
must be close.

'Do you know a fence with wire circles running across the
top?' she whispers. 'I cut my hands on it.'

'Where were you?' Rory asks.

'Shh,' Vic gestures. 'Go on.'

'It's the fence from my dream.' She tells them about the newspaper stand. 'All these scratches appeared when I was drawing. Look how many there are.' Evie can't stop turning her hands over and over. 'We have to find the fence.'

Vic nods and Rory leaves the room.

'Does Rory know where it is?'

'He's just checking something, Evie,' replies Vic. 'He'll be back in a minute. Hopefully with the first aid kit, too.'

Evie looks at her dad. He is covering his mouth. She can see his lips trembling even though he presses his hand hard against them.

She uncurls her fingers and puts her hand in his. 'They don't hurt,' she says to him.

'I'm so sorry,' he chokes. 'Tell me if you've had enough. I'll take you home tonight if you want. You don't have to –'

'It won't stop this,' Evie says. 'I know that now.'

'I wish . . . I just don't understand.'

'My hands are a sign, Dad. It's not meant to frighten us. Okay? She's leading me to where I'm meant to go.'

'Jesus Christ,' he moans.

Rory comes back in with a folder and some bandages. He shows something to Vic, who nods in agreement.

'Evie, have a look at this.' Rory passes her a photo. 'It's taken near the Keswick terminal.'

Evie studies a photo of a corrugated iron warehouse. At the back of the picture is a fence with barbed wire circles running across the top.

'Here's a better one,' Rory says.

The photo is passed around the room. Theo and Nick shrug; it means nothing to them.

'What do you think, Evie?' asks Vic.

'It could be it. It certainly looks like it.' Evie passes the pictures back. 'I think we should go there.'

'I'll organise a car,' says Vic.

The detectives leave the room.

'You're quiet, Theo.'

He looks up at her, trying to smile.

'I'm okay,' Evie says.

Silence.

'I'm getting closer.'

They drive towards West Terrace back out to the Mile End area.

'Okay, Evie, let's retrace Athena's steps,' Vic says from the front seat. 'We're pretty sure she went to the festival, which is situated here.' He gestures out the window.

Rory turns off the main road into an adjoining street.

'Presuming they went by either car or foot,' continues Vic, 'this is most likely the way they would've come.'

They turn into an industrial eyesore. Warehouse after warehouse, kilometres of wire fencing and the lack of trees make it hard to differentiate one street from the next.

'Around this corner is where the picture was taken,' says Rory, stopping the car.

'No,' Evie says with complete confidence. 'This isn't right.'

'What?' the detectives chime.

'This isn't the place,' she repeats.

'Why don't you get out of the car and look?' says Rory.

'We're here now,' encourages Vic.

'I'd be wasting your time,' Evie tells them. 'Look, there are fences everywhere. None of them are the right one though, not here. I don't mean to sound rude, Vic, but surely there are other fences like this in the area?'

The detectives look at each other. Vic nods and Rory turns the car around just a bit too fast. Gravel sprays up, hitting the window. Evie hears his perfect teeth grind.

'Just tell us when to stop,' he mutters.

Rory drives over the railway track to the western side of the road. Evie hears the tyres – *click, bump, click, bump.* She holds her hands tightly. They're so close now.

'Stop!'

Evie spots the trees before the fence. To her they're simply four triangles, standing tall. Unmistakable. She's opening the door before the car has even stopped and running towards the fence.

'What are these?' she calls, treading on silver lines wedged into the road.

'Old railway lines.' Rory jogs behind her. 'There used to be a terminal here for the mills.'

'So simple,' she laughs.

The wire fence borders a carpark lined with trucks and vans.

Evie looks around, sniffing the air.

'What?' says Rory.

'There's that smell.'

Rory leans against the fence and sniffs. 'What smell?'

'That smell.'

'I can't smell anything except fumes from one of the factories.'

'No, it's like grass that's been mowed, something like that.' She inhales deeply. 'It reminds me of a farm. Yeah, it's a farmy smell.'

'You couldn't be further from a farm,' replies Rory.

'But that's where she is.'

'A farm?'

'I don't know. I just know the smell and I know it's connected to her.' Evie gestures around them. 'It's all connected to her,' she adds.

Rory sighs and walks back to the car.

'It's not my fault,' she shrugs, following him.

The others stand around. Vic stubs out his cigarette. 'Anything?'

'She thinks Athena's at a farm.'

'What?'

'I didn't say she was at a farm, Rory,' Evie corrects. 'I said the farm smell is connected to her.'

Rory gets back into the driver's seat and slams the door.

'What are you two going on about?' Vic mutters.

'Vic, I need to – to just be here for a while by myself.'

Vic stares at her.

'Moo,' she says to him.

'Huh?'

'Look, Vic, take Dad and Theo and go for a drive. Just go away for a while. I need some space. Every time I turn around one of you's there.'

Rory starts the engine as the men get in the car.

Nick winds down the window. 'Are you sure you're okay? We won't go far.'

'Dad, I'm fine.'

At last the car disappears down the road. Linking her fingers around the curve of her grandmother's bangles Evie stands by the four trees.

'Ok,' she says, calmly brushing her hand along the pine needles. 'Follow the signs.'

No one is around. It's so quiet, so desolate. Carefully Evie walks further up the road, hearing her shoes crunch along the gravel. Above, a lone crow calls 'caw, caw' and inside her head a gentle humming starts.

At the end of the road stands a narrow bridge. As Evie gets closer she sees it's not an actual bridge but rather a network of overhead pipes that run along and connect with something on the other side. Her eyes follow their convoluted journey and there she discovers the missing part of the puzzle. Three cylindrical towers, taller than anything else around. She lifts her hand to her throat. 'What a place to be,' she murmurs.

Crouching down on the footpath, Evie buries her head in her lap. She can hear her heart pounding and her breath loud in her throat. She can hear Victoria's words, soothing, guiding, but what she feels is like nothing before. It suffocates her soul, leaving an emptiness void of any care or love, and a fear so deep, so black, it crushes any chance of hope. Every cell in her body feels it – Athena is here, waiting, all alone. Evie wraps her arms around her chest and gently rocks herself.

'I'm sorry it took me so long,' she cries.

The three towers stand alone, stark against the wasteland. The wind begins to moan and the four pines bend and shiver. In the air a whisper floats, 'So, so, so.' Gradually the sound becomes louder, crisper. 'So cold,' it cries. 'So cold. So cold. So alone.'

Evie is back by the fence when the car returns. Her dad goes to her, anxiety pasted all over his face.

'I know where she is.' Evie points to the towers.

'Up there?' says Nick.

Evie nods. 'She's inside.'

'Are you –?'

'Yes. You tell them.'

'Vic?' Nick clears his throat. 'Evie says she's up there.'

'What? The wheat silos?'

'That's right.'

They stand there, their arms folded. Tension all around. Evie goes and sits in the car. Outside she hears them arguing.

'How could she have got up there, Nick?'

'I don't know! But that's where Evie says she is.'

'That's bloody ridiculous!'

'Well, that's what you got her out here for, Vic.'

'Fifteen minutes ago she said she thought the girl was on a farm.'

'She was trying to identify a smell, Rory. Look – wheat, farm. Theo and I understand how this works. You don't.'

'So what?' Vic yells. 'You think we should drain everything out of the silos because of that?'

'You prick,' Nick spits.

'Come on, guys.' Theo stands between them. 'Stay calm. Come on, Nicky.'

'You got us over here,' Nick growls. 'You made my daughter think you had faith in her. And now you're just going to come to your own fucking conclusion?'

'I understand this is difficult for you,' begins Vic.

'Difficult? Difficult?' Nick fights to get closer but Theo holds him back. 'You don't know what difficult is, mate. She has to live with this for the rest of her life. Do you understand that? Evie has trusted you, Vic. She has – she has let you in on something that makes her so, so vulnerable. My wife, her mother, is sick with fear of what this'll do to her. Do you have any idea how this must feel for her, for us, for our family? I'm not letting this happen, do you hear?'

Vic stares at the ground. 'I'm sorry, Nick. I can't get a warrant to search the silos unless we have some evidence.'

'Well, do your job and find some.'

Nick walks back to the car and slams the door.

They drive back to the hotel in silence. Evie has never seen her father so angry. His face is contorted and his eyes are dark. She wants to say something to him. She wants to make him better but they're so past that now. She will leave him to Theo. Theo will know how to handle him.

Before Evie gets out she leans over to the front passenger seat. 'Vic?'

'Yes, Evie?' he sighs.

'There is evidence there. You just have to find it. Look around the four pine trees. It's hidden there somewhere.'

In the bathroom Evie takes Athena's red cardigan out of her bag. She rubs it against her face, the wool soft and smooth on her skin. In the mirror she looks pale: the hollowness of her sockets reflect dark shadows underneath. Her left eye is red and puffy. Her bottom lip is swollen where she keeps biting it and tiny cracks at the side of her mouth are opening into sores. She turns her hands over, watching the scratches, like tiny comets shooting in all directions. The knot at the back of her head is so matted now she can only hide it in a bun. For the first time in days she touches it. It's still wet and sticky.

'How have I come to this?'

But Evie knows the price is small.

Tomorrow they are returning to Sydney. As soon as they got back to the hotel Nick booked tickets on an early flight. In sixteen hours Evie will be home. Back to Alex and to Poppy, whom she hasn't seen in two weeks. Back to the Glebe markets where Petrina will hug her and Ben's crooked smile will only make her laugh. Back to Seb, who keeps her secret. Home, where everything will be different. Everything, because Evie understands she is different now.

The men watch the seven o'clock news. Evie lies curled up on her bed, the red cardigan resting on her shoulders. She won't write anything to Athena, not tonight. It hurts so much when she thinks of Athena's family and their pain at losing their firstborn. Their daughter.

Evie closes her eyes and hums a lullaby her mother used to sing when she'd had a bad dream. 'Sweet and low, sweet and low, Wind of the western sea.'

Evie is lying in her parents' bed. Her mother's arms are wrapped around her, her fingers gently stroking her hair. 'Low, low, breathe and blow, Wind of the western sea.' Her mother's breath smells sweet, like milk and honey. 'Mamma's here,' she whispers. 'You're safe now. There are no monsters behind the door. Just fairies.' Her eyes feel heavier as her mother's song guides her into sleep.

Evie sits up in the hotel bed. 'Dad?' she calls. 'I think I'd like to call Mum.'

In Theo's room she dials the number. Robin is home now, waiting for them.

'Nick, is that you?'

'It's me, Evie.'

'Evie!'

Silence.

'Evie, are you still there?'

'Yes.'

'I don't, I don't –'

'Mum, it's okay.'

'No. No, it's not,' she squeaks.

Evie can picture her mother curled up on the lounge, a glass of red wine in her hand.

'I'm so proud of you,' she splutters. 'I want you to know that. There are things we need to talk about. Things that happened a long time ago. But I did what I thought was best.'

'The best for who, Mum?'

Silence.

'I've tried to be a good mum. I know I don't do a very good job sometimes.'

'Were you scared? Is that what it was?'

'I was frightened for you. I wanted everything to be perfect,' she sighs. 'I wanted you to have what I didn't have – love, stability.'

'What about honesty?'

Silence except for her mother's breath.

'I just wanted to protect you,' she finally says.

'This is the way I am, Mum.'

'I know. I know, Evie, and I don't know what I'd do if anything ever happened to you. I keep thinking about that poor family. We'll just take it slowly, you and me.'

'I want to go back to school, Mum. I don't really know what I'm going to do but I want to go back. I know that. I just want things to be normal. Normal between all of us.' Evie wipes the tears on her sleeve. 'Well, as normal as they can be.'

'You sound different, Evie.'

'I am.'

He drags her off the fence and holds her hand tightly, the cuts stinging under his sweat. He yells and slaps her face over and over. He holds her cheeks and pulls her lips apart as he screams in her face, his spit flying into her eyes and mouth. He pushes her. The back of her head connects with something hard. She holds the pain; it feels wet and sticky. There's blood on her fingers. She goes to speak but he pushes her again and again until everything goes black. Black. He carries her to the tower but she's a dead weight. Instead he drags her by the legs, her head and body bumping up each metal stair. He forces the door open, props her in the entrance and pushes her in. She falls down, down into the darkness, until the thud. Millions of tiny wheat grains fly up in the air then slowly, slowly settle on her face and mouth.

Evie waits for the 6 a.m wake up call. Outside the darkness is turning into a misty grey. She hears the brakes of a truck as it starts and stops at each garbage bin.

Tonight Alex will come over and they'll lie on her bed and she'll tell her things, not everything. They'll find something to laugh about. They always do.

At last the phone rings. The recorded message speaks: 'At the third stroke, it will be five fifty-nine and seven seconds.'

'Are you awake?' her dad asks.

'Yes.'

'I'll put the kettle on.'

They have a cup of tea, shower, pack and are in a taxi on the way to the airport by 7 a.m.

Theo brings the bags back from the check-in desk. 'The flight's delayed an hour due to morning fog. Let's get a coffee.'

They sit around, not saying much. The airport café is crowded with glum-faced morning travellers. Evie picks at a toasted sandwich and Theo spills sugar on the table. Nick stares out the window at the fog.

'A watched pot never boils,' Theo tells him.

'I won't be sad if I never see Adelaide airport again.'

Theo passes Nick the paper. 'You should read this letter to the editor.'

'Later,' he says. 'Evie, have you done your eyedrops this morning?'

Evie starts rummaging through her bag. The bandages on her hands make her clumsy.

'Give it to me. I'll find them.' Nick's mobile rings. 'Hang on a sec.'

Theo peers up from the paper. Evie listens to her dad speak. She knows who's on the other end.

'How? But when did this happen? Shit! Yes, okay. We're at the airport. Yes. Yes.'

'Who was that?' Theo asks.

'Vic.'

'What did he want?' Theo snarls.

'Evie?'

'Yes, Dad.'

'They've found some evidence.'

'You're kidding!' shouts Theo, scrunching up the newspaper.

'Vic went back on his way home from work,' he tells them. 'Something made him want to look around those pine trees. He said it was pretty late but he had a torch. He scratched about in the dirt, gave the trees a shake and bingo, a nest fell out.'

'What sort of nest?'

'A bloody bird's nest, Theo.' Nick shakes his head. 'He was going to his daughter's for dinner, so he took it to show his grandson. He had a bit to drink and ended up staying the night. This morning Vic and his grandson were having a look at the nest when the kid pulls something out from the very bottom of it.'

'And?' Theo says.

'It was a piece of red silk with gold and black threads. It's from the jacket Athena wore that night.'

Theo snaps his fingers. 'The jacket from Evie's dream!'

'Vic said it was amazing seeing the nest was so small.'

'Vic thought *that* was the amazing bit?'

'They're sending a patrol car, Evie.'

'I know.'

The road is taped off. Twenty to thirty police in dark-blue overalls comb the area. Some are looking in the carpark, some dig in the grass along the fence and where the four pine trees stand. A smaller group stand at the bottom of the tower stairs. They look like they're being given instructions. Vic is smoking and talking to a man with 'FORENSIC' written on the back of his coat. Rory can't stop showing his perfect teeth.

Athena's uncle and father stand alone at the end of the road. Evie doesn't know what she's going to say to them. There are no words for this.

'Here,' she says, pulling the red cardigan out of her bag.

Mr Poulos's hand trembles as he takes it from her.

'Thank you,' he chokes.

'No. Thank you,' she whispers and goes back to her father.

The men in blue overalls climb to the top of the silo tower. Their boots clang on each step. When they reach the top they talk for a while, then two of the men pull at the handle of the door. It groans as they slide it open. They disappear inside.

Theo cups his hands around her shoulders and squeezes them.

The mobile is pressed to Nick's ear. 'They're in there now. I'll call back as soon as we know something.' He shakes his head over and over. 'No, Robin, no cameras, no journos. It's only us and the police. I know. I know. I'll tell her. Yes, I'll tell her.'

'Mum?'

'Yeah. She's in a bit of a state.'

'She feels far way,' Evie says, sinking back into her father's chest. He wraps his arms around her, holding her tight. Through her spine she feels his heart beating.

'Our wise, strong, precious girl,' he whispers. The words land on her skin. 'You believed in yourself, Evie. When there was doubt everywhere you held on. You've handled this with such dignity and, as your mum just said, that's about as proud as a parent can get.' She breathes them in.

They wait and watch the entrance to the tower. Finally a police officer emerges from the doorway. He looks over at Vic and puts his thumb up. Vic nods. 'They've found her.'

Evie touches her throat. It feels soft. She swallows and the saliva slips gently down. She closes her eyes, the burden lifting from her body. And in the distance she hears the words:

Like one, that on a lonesome road
Doth walk in fear and dread,
And having once turned round walks on,
And turns no more his head.

'Thank you,' she says.

There are reports to fill in and statements to sign. Police headquarters is a buzz of handshakes and backslapping. Men and women in uniform and plain clothes echo their congratulations through the corridors. 'Well done, Vic', 'On ya, Van de Meer'. Occasionally they steal a glance at Evie.

And Evie watches them. She doesn't share their feelings. She feels sad. Sad for Athena's parents, sad for Melena and sad for the uncle, Con Poulos, who gently led the grieving father away. Evie can still see the way his shoulders slumped and his back trembled with the realisation that their search and hope for Athena, their firstborn, was over.

Theo takes the seat next to Evie. She covers her nose. He must've just slapped on more aftershave.

'Well, we got on another flight.'

'Hmm?'

'We got on a flight. Ten past four.'

'Good.'

'You okay?'

'I will be,' answers Evie. 'As soon as I get out of here.'

'They see it differently to us.'

'How can they?'

'Well, be grateful you're still classified a juvenile or we'd be stuck here for days.'

'So there is something good about being underage,' Evie groans. 'Remind me to tell Alex that.'

'You're looking forward to seeing her, hey?'

'Yeah. Big time.'

'Apparently they're releasing a media statement at four-thirty. We'll be safely in the sky. That's why your dad's taking so long. He's going over it for the one thousandth time to check there's no mention of you, or your mother will eat him for breakfast.'

Evie frowns.

'Don't worry. There isn't.'

'Poor Mum and Dad. What a thing I've put them through.'

'Hey, they're really proud of you, girl.'

'Yeah.'

'And just between you and me, your grandma would be, too.'

O nce more Evie fastens her belt and grips the seat as the plane bumps and lifts through the cloud cover. She gazes out at the sky, blue and endless, almost expecting to see Athena fly past and wave like something out of *The Wizard of Oz*. She giggles just for that second. She knows Athena is with her family at last.

Theo and Nick are two seats in front. Theo's aftershave wafts through the cabin. He must be snoring, as every now and then Nick looks over and nudges him.

Evie takes out her sketchpad and reads the last entry, thinking how long ago it seems she wrote those words and how far she has come since then.

Opening a fresh page and smoothing down the surface Evie writes:

Friday 7 July.
Dear Athena,
I'm on my way home and so are you.
Well, we both managed to stick to the deal. In the last seven days I have learnt more about myself than in the sixteen and a half years I've been alive. If it wasn't for you finding me or the red cardigan finding Dad, whichever way you look at it, I'd still be trapped inside my old self. Now it's like I've met my real self. I'm trying on my new skin and it fits. Fits pretty well, too! Thank you for helping me find it and thank you for comforting me yesterday. I could feel your calm energy around me. I still can.

I understand I'll always feel different but that's okay. I am, and maybe I like feeling that way. Maybe I don't want to be like everyone else, even though I used to think I did.

I'm like Grandma and everybody loved her and as Dad says they thought she was special and she was. She wasn't bad or weird – she was just normal. Maybe that's another reason I don't feel scared any more.

It's weird. I don't feel scared about going back to school. I don't feel scared about facing Powell or any of those girls. There's nothing special about them. I feel a bit nervous about seeing Seb (haven't decided if I'm going to tell Alex) but I think those nerves might be butterflies, if you know what I mean. And I think I'm even brave enough to continue with my drawing elective. I said 'I think'!

I might be going off a bit early, so much is buzzing through my head. I mean, who's to say I'll never be scared again but at least it'll be about what's out there, not what's in here, in me. So thank you. Hey, it's pretty cool talking to you.

I know things will be better at home. It'll take a while but at least we're all honest now and that'll make a big difference, not just to me and Mum but to Mum and Dad, too. So that's got to be a good thing.

The food's coming down the aisle and I'm starving. Dad keeps looking around. I just gave him a little wave but I better go.

And if I had to go through it all again to get to this (if there really wasn't an easier way, that is), would I?, Yes, I'd go through it all again. I think!

Forever, Evie x

Acknowledgements

Senior Constable Denis Blowes from the South Australian Police

Con Bourliofas

David Burke

Margaret Burke

Eva Mills, Commissioning Editor, Random House

Catherine Steuart

Tara Wynne, Curtis Brown Australia

Josie, clairvoyant, formerly of Bayview, NSW

And as always Victoria, Nicholas and Michael

About the author

J. C. Burke was born in Sydney in 1965, the fourth of five daughters. With writers for parents, she grew up in a world full of noise, drama and books, and the many colourful characters who came to visit provided her with an endless supply of stories and impersonations.

Burke decided to become a nurse after her mother lost a long battle with cancer. She trained at Royal Prince Alfred Hospital in Sydney and later specialised in the field of Oncology, working in Haematology and Bone Marrow Transplant Units in Australia and the UK. A creative writing course at Sydney University led to a mentorship with Gary Crew and the publication in 2002 of her first novel, *White Lies* (Lothian), a CBC Notable Book.

J. C. Burke lives on Sydney's Northern Beaches with her husband and two children. She does a lot of yoga and a bit of nursing. She loves writing for children and young adults, as they still have an optimistic eye on the world.

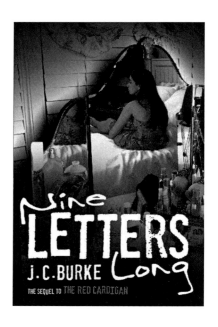

Nine Letters Long

Don't miss the thrilling sequel to *The Red Cardigan* . . .

Evie has a gift – a gift she's not always comfortable with. But when Poppy suggests they conduct a séance, Evie reluctantly agrees. The letters on the board start spelling out one name – C-A-Z – over and over, and Evie knows she's been contacted again. A cryptic message leads Evie to a family where two sisters, one living, one dead, share a dark secret that must be revealed. But is Evie strong enough to solve the mystery and reveal the truth in time to release both girls?

Available now at all good retailers